AUBRIE DIONNE

I started writing because my flute students urged me to publish the stories I made up in their lessons. My books are influenced by my undying love of Star Wars and Star Trek, and by my own musical life. When I'm not writing, I teach flute and play in orchestras.

You can follow me on Twitter @AuthorAubrie.

GW00725868

A Diva in Manhattan

AUBRIE DIONNE

HarperImpulse an imprint of
HarperCollinsPublishers Ltd
77–85 Fulham Palace Road
Hammersmith, London W6 8JB

www.harpercollins.co.uk

A Paperback Original 2014

First published in Great Britain in ebook format by HarperImpulse 2014

Cover images © Shutterstock.com

Aubrine Dionne asserts the moral right
to be identified as the author of this work

A catalogue record for this book is
available from the British Library

ISBN: 9780008124038

*To Donna Lombardo, the fabulous
opera soprano and my good friend.
Thank you for all of your insights and advice!*

CHAPTER ONE

First Sight

Alaina sang the last note of her aria and waited for her voice to echo throughout the farthest rows of the Metropolitan Opera House. A year ago, she would have never thought she'd be standing here in front of the judges. But, one favorable review on her Italian tour last summer was all it had taken to escalate her into high demand status and get her the audition of a lifetime for the character of Pamina in *The Magic Flute*.

She brought her arms down to her sides and awaited judgment. She'd sung her lungs out. If that wasn't the bomb, then she didn't know what they were looking for.

Roxanne Smith, an older woman with Elizabeth Taylor's wild dark hair, and the president of the board nodded to the European conductor, Altez Vior, then addressed Alaina. "Obviously you have the vocals for the part."

Alaina concealed her breath of relief and bowed her head, trying to look modest - an act that didn't come to her naturally. "Thank you."

"But." Elizabeth's look-a-like tapped her pen on her cheek.

Alaina swallowed her disdain. She never did like those old

movies. "Yes?"

"The role calls for a sweet young maiden in love, which is hardly what you're known for."

Alaina bit back a retort. "I can assure you, I'm an excellent actress."

Roxanne held up a finger. "But will concert goers want to see you in that role? Will they believe you are capable of unrequited love?"

"They will believe what I sing." She was at the top of her game, and she'd have the audience at her feet with one sweet note. Why couldn't these idiots see that?

The conductor, nodded, rubbing his hand over his crazy white hair. "Perhaps. But, to get them in the seats in the first place, you need to soften your image."

Alaina scoffed. Her image? Why, she was the most beautiful, alluring, and versatile soprano around. Who else were they looking for? Mother Teresa? "And how do you propose I do that?"

Roxanne smiled wickedly. "We want you to volunteer as a music teacher at Heart House."

"Heart House?" Shock weakened her knees, followed by a large dose of fear. That was a charter school for the underprivileged. They scribbled more graffiti on the walls than notes on a page. She'd even heard there were gangs.

Mr. Vior nodded. "That's not all. You'll have to attend a number of high profile fundraisers for children with disabilities, victims of tragedies, and the Center for Cancer Research."

Alaina blinked as she digested his words. Being an only child, she had no practice working with children, the only tragic thing she'd experienced was a bad review, and the thought of anything medical made her sick to her stomach. "I see."

The conductor raised both his eyebrows. "If you agree, we are willing to offer you the part."

The bright lights burned into her retinas as a feeling of claustrophobia came over her. For someone who'd been on stage her entire life, social work was far from her comfort zone.

2

She couldn't refuse. Singing at the Met would propel her career into the stratosphere. She'd never need to belt out another Ava Maria at a wedding again. She could handpick any role she wanted, join any touring opera company in the country, maybe even the world.

"I accept."

"Excellent." Roxanne clapped her iPad case closed and stood. "We'll see you tonight at our first fundraiser for Project Wish."

Tonight? She'd been planning on a bubble bath to de-stress. Before she could respond, the conductor walked to the stage and shook her hand. "I look forward to working with you."

All Alaina could manage was "mmhmm."

I got the part. She kept repeating that phrase as she slipped on her faux fur coat. She almost forgot her green snakeskin Gucci purse on stage and had to run back for it. She felt like a deer caught in the headlights of a monster truck.

She could sing the part easily enough, but could she teach inner city ruffians? Comfort children with disabilities? Rub elbows with cancer survivors? Compassion was something she reserved for the tragic characters in her arias. In real life, she'd never so much as poured a bowl of Campbell's at a soup kitchen. She hadn't had the time. Her parents had her practicing and acting since the age of five when she appeared singing the theme song in an Oscar Mayer ad.

Alaina stumbled into the traffic choked streets of New York, wishing she hadn't fired her limo driver back in Italy when he'd gotten lost. She raised her hand to hail a cab, but at rush hour, it was like swimming against the tide in a sea of sharks.

As she waited on the curb, drills echoed from across West 65th street. A construction crew tore up the sidewalk.

Honestly, did they have to work at this time of day?

She narrowed her eyes, about to shoot lasers at them for disturbing her peace, when a man caught her attention. Holding a giant plank of wood like it was a golf club, he reached up and handed it to three men on the scaffolding.

Had Hercules come down from the heavens?

The man was tall with broad shoulders, wearing a light blue shirt and jeans. Dark brown hair curled under his hard hat. He had a strong jawline and stood as though he owned the street.

He turned toward her, froze in place, and tipped his hard hat as if saying hello. With the angle of the sun, she could barely make out his face, the hat casting most of it in shadow. Surely, he wasn't addressing her.

A car beeped rudely in front of her and Alaina jumped. "Holy batshit! What the hell?"

"You gonna get in or not, lady?" A cab driver shouted through the passenger window.

Alaina looked for another cab, preferably one with a nicer driver. No luck.

She sighed and muttered under her breath, "Beggars can't be choosers."

Only when she'd plopped inside did she remember to look out the window for the construction guy, but a large bus had pulled up beside the cab, blocking her view. A young boy stuck his tongue on the window and wiggled his fingers over both ears.

Lovely. Just one more reason to stay away from kids.

What was she doing anyway? Those construction workers were all grunts who drank beer, whistled at women, and watched sports on TV. Any relationship with one of them would last all of two seconds.

Alaina sighed, playing with the ring on her finger. One of these days she'd meet her match.

***

"You're more likely to fly a green pig to Mars than meet the likes of her."

Brett ignored his friend and watched the woman slip into the cab, awestruck. Her hair shone like a sunset on fire, reminding him of the many times he'd sit with his father on the side of Saddleback Mountain and watch the evening spread over the valley of forest below their log cabin.

The woman's fox like features were both alluring and innocent, like she'd lived in a bubble her whole life. The way her fur coat clung to her shapely body stirred urges within him that he hadn't felt in a long time. He hadn't wanted anything since the fire, not like the way he wanted her.

The cab drove away, and the familiar ache of loss settled in his gut. He'd probably never see her again. "Who do you reckon she is?"

Phil shrugged and picked up his drill. He was fifteen years older than Brett with graying hair and thick wrinkles around his eyes. "Probably some opera diva from the Met with a stick up her ass the size of a flagpole."

His friend started drilling, and Brett searched the curb where she'd stood. Opera? He'd never see an opera in his entire life. All he could think of was Vikings screaming at the top of their lungs and a conductor wearing a powdered wig waving his arms around. Not the most enjoyable pastime.

Phil stopped drilling and reached for another nail. He glanced up at Brett with an apologetic expression, as if he hadn't realized how far he'd fallen. "A man can dream, right?"

Brett shrugged, trying to push away this sudden urge to find her. He hadn't dreamt about anything in a long time. Not since he'd left Maine to start over in the big city, where very little reminded him of the home he'd left behind. Except her sunset hair.

Get moving. Stay on the job.

Construction kept his mind busy, kept him from thinking about the past. He walked over to the loading truck and pulled out another plank of wood. The other guys complained about their backs, so he always took the heavy lifting jobs. Compared to logging, this was a piece of cake.

Brett hefted the plank onto his shoulder and carried it to the guys on the scaffolding.

His supervisor, Al Higgins, came over with one eye on his clipboard. "Time for a dinner break."

"I'm not hungry." Brett placed the plank down on the curb. The last thing he wanted to do was sit down and stew over his life. "Give it to someone else."

Al tucked his clipboard under his arm. "Brett, you're a hard worker, and I like that. But, everyone needs to eat sometime." He gestured for two other men to pick up the plank.

Brett crossed his arms. "I'd rather finish unloading."

Al pulled him aside. "To tell you the truth, I'd rather you did, too. You can unload those planks faster than any two men here. But, you know how it is. Government regulations and such."

Brett nodded. He didn't want to get his supervisor in trouble just because he couldn't be left alone with his own memories. "Got it." He picked up his lunch bag from the giant cooler his team all shared and took a seat on the curb.

Biting into his ham sandwich, he studied the grand building the woman had come out of. Maybe he should see an opera sometime. A comic opera - not something tragic. He'd had enough of that.

A limo with the license plate DeBarr pulled up to the curb, and an older woman in black velvet stepped out while talking on the phone. Her gray hair was cropped around her face in small curls. "Don't tell me you have another conflict!"

Brett tried not to eavesdrop, but her commanding voice cut through the construction noise and the honking cars. He glanced away, pretending to be interested in the passing traffic and took another bite of his sandwich.

"Project Wish is counting on you. You were going to be the biggest bid of the night." She huffed, pacing back and forth as the limo waited in the fire lane.

Brett swallowed another bite. Someone was going to get a ticket.

"Fine." The old woman hung up and stashed her phone in a fuzzy leopard purse. She turned to get back into the limo when

6

she caught his gaze and looked him up and down. Her features changed from irritated to intrigued. "You, over there. Are you single?"

Was she hitting on him? Brett stashed the rest of his sandwich in the bag. "Me?"

"No, the other three hunks eating a sandwich." She walked over and reached for his left hand. "Well, you're not married, and you look like you'll fit in the tux I have in the trunk."

One more breath and she'd be asking him to marry her. Brett stood and crumpled up his sandwich bag. "Listen, I have to get back to work."

He turned to leave, and she placed her hand on his arm. "I have an offer you won't refuse."

Man, she had a grip like a python. Brett glanced at her wrinkled, boney hand, bejeweled in all types of diamond and gem rings. Only a shmuck would pull his arm away from an old woman. He'd have to convince her there were other fish in the sea. "Although you are beautiful, you're not my type."

She laughed as if he was ridiculous. "This is hardly for me. It's for Project Wish."

He scratched his head as anxiousness raised the hairs on the back of his neck. He had to get back to work. Chances were, the other guys hadn't volunteered to unload the truck, and they needed those planks for the next phase of the project. But the intensity in her eyes made him wonder. "Project Wish?"

"A nonprofit agency who lends aid to people who've lost everything in natural disasters like hurricanes, floods, fires…"

"Fires?"

She nodded. "Yes."

A sharp ache spread inside him. Images of his family's log cabin in flames roared in his thoughts. Brett blinked them away. If he could help someone else who'd experienced such loss. "What do you want me to do?"

She leaned in and dropped her voice. "I need someone to take the place of my son. He was supposed to attend this fundraiser tonight. It's an annual auction to raise money for Project Wish."

So her son stood her up. Brett could understand her frustration, but inviting someone from off the street seemed a bit rash. "Can't you go by yourself?"

She shook her head, and her diamond earrings dangled like pendulums. "No. He was on the auctioning block."

"Auctioning block?" This did not sound good. Brett glanced back to the construction site. No one seemed to miss him yet.

"A one night dinner date with for two: him and the lucky lady whose purse is big enough to win the bid."

"You mean you want me to pose as your son, dress up, put myself on the auction block, and take the winner out to dinner?"

She crossed her arms and narrowed her eyes as if she'd underestimated him. "That's right. And I'll pay for every cent."

"I don't know." The whole idea seemed too outlandish for someone who liked his world kept simple.

"Please, I won't be able to find anyone else on such short notice, and it is for charity."

A charity he believed in. Brett sighed as he considered what it would feel like to put on a tux and schmooze with all the hoity toities of New York. "My shift doesn't end until seven."

She clapped her hands together. "Perfect. That's when the cocktails start."

He ran his hands through his hair as apprehension tightened in his chest. "I'm not good at small talk. I've lived most of my life up in a log cabin in the middle of nowhere."

She pointed a finger at him. "You're smarter than you let on. Besides, it's not like anyone your age has the money to win the bid. You'll probably be taking out some old spinster like me for coffee. Believe me, you'll be fine."

Brett knew he was in too far over his head. But, he couldn't ignore an organization like Project Wish. And it wasn't like he was looking forward to a night alone with his thoughts to keep him

8

company. This woman was pushy, but he found her sass endearing. She reminded him of a cross between his own grandmother and Rose from the Golden Girls. Not that he watched the reruns. Well, maybe sometimes he did.

"Okay." He nodded slowly, convincing himself in the process. "Count me in."

CHAPTER TWO

Tea

Alaina straightened her red, Valentino lace dress and walked into the lobby of the Met. The board had decorated the dual spiral staircases with roses, and the who's who of New York mingled holding glasses of champagne.

She wanted her own glass of bubbly while soaking naked in lilac scented water. But no, here she was in this snoozefest raising money for…what was Project Wish anyway?

"Alaina, so nice of you to come." Altez Vior took her hand and kissed the back.

Alaina smiled despite the irritation rising within her. *I'm only here because you held a knife to my throat.* "Anything to ensure the opera goes well."

The conductor glanced around the room. "There are a few people I'd like to you meet, namely the founders of Project Wish, along with the other members of the board."

She swallowed a yawn. "I can't wait."

Worry crossed his face as he scanned the crowd. "We're missing Grace DeBarr, the largest donor for both Project Wish and the opera. I wonder if something held her up."

Opportunity rang in Alaina's ears. This was her excuse to make herself scarce. "Maybe you should call her, just in case."

"Of course." He checked his watch. "Excuse me."

"Absolutely." She ushered him toward the coatroom. As he dug in his coat for his cell phone, she slipped back into the crowd.

Now where were those appetizers?

The front door opened, and an older woman in black velvet walked in with the hottest date Alaina had ever seen. Dressed in a sleek, black Armani suit, this man towered a head above most with wide shoulders, a square jaw, and perfectly rugged features that oozed masculinity. Long, luscious waves of dark brown hair were slicked back from his face, curling around his ears. Dark brown eyes simmered as he scanned the room. He settled on her and interest sparked in his gaze.

Too bad he was a gold digger preying on an older woman who should know better.

Alaina elbowed a man in his fifties picking an egg roll off a waiter's tray. "Who's that lovely couple?"

He popped the egg roll in his mouth and stepped toward her. His eyes rolled over the spots on her dress where the bare skin showed through the lace. "That's Grace DeBarr, the richest woman in New York and one of the project's biggest donors."

She didn't care if he gawked, as long as he provided information. "And who's the arm candy?"

The man frowned as if shocked by her bluntness. Or was he jealous of her interest in the other man? "I'm not sure. Her son is scheduled for the auction block at eight. I suppose that's him."

"Her son?" Alaina searched the older woman's face for even a fraction of that hotness but found no resemblance. What did it matter as long as he wasn't her date?

Mr. Egg Roll provided his hand. "Alan Hardy, vice president of the board. And you are?"

She took his hand and dropped it after one shake. "Alaina Amaldi. I'm sorry. There's something I have to be getting to…"

She turned and cut through the crowd.

Mrs. DeBarr had found the conductor, and the two of them were chatting up a storm. Alaina turned around and hid behind a waiter. She couldn't get caught up in that conversation right now. Not when there was a hot guy walking around without a date. Her evening just got a whole hell of a lot more interesting.

Mr. Hottie stood alone and aloof by the punch table.

Alaina had a sudden craving for punch. She leaned over and reached for the serving spoon, making sure her breasts were on full display as her diamond pendant dangled over the pink liquid.

She had to use her attributes to her advantage. Long ago, she gave up trying to be pencil thin and went down the curvy route. Those models could nibble on lettuce, but a lyric soprano needed a hearty meal to belt out those high A's.

She dipped the large serving spoon in and trickled the liquid in her glass. She glanced over in his direction and -sure enough- caught him staring.

Alaina raised an eyebrow as she sipped her drink, leaving red lipstick on the rim. She wished she could leave some on his cleanly shaven cheek. "Enjoying your evening?"

He shrugged uncomfortably. For someone with a billion- dollar inheritance, he seemed like a country bumpkin out of his element. "I just got here."

Alaina stepped forward, claiming the space beside him. "Yes, I saw you come in with your...mother?"

He stuck his hands in his pockets and glanced around the room as if spies were lurking everywhere. "Yes, my...mother."

He wasn't a conversation starter, that's for certain. But, Alaina found his reluctance delightful. So many sleaze balls openly hit on her and this guy was playing hard to get.

She curled her toes in her heels. A challenge. She liked that.

"Alaina Amaldi." She offered her hand.

He took his hand out of his pocket. "Lance DeBarr."

His skin was warm and dry, his hands rough with calluses. Why would someone as rich as him have calluses?

"So, I hear you're on the auction block tonight."

He rolled his eyes. "Please, don't remind me."

"Your mother put you up to it?"

"You could say that."

She wiggled her eyebrows. "What are they auctioning you for?"

Was that a blush in his cheeks? This guy was so damn cute.

"A dinner date for two."

"Oh." Had she brought the checkbook? Perhaps she'd want to make a bid. All in the name of charity, of course. She still didn't know which charity, but that didn't matter. "So you're afraid one of these older ladies will buy you off and you'll have to spend your night talking about knitting and tea?"

He leaned in and smiled. "Maybe I like tea."

Was he flirting? Alaina trailed her finger across the pocket of his suit. "I'm a black tea type of gal."

He raised his eyebrows. "So you like it strong?"

"Strong and dark." Man this party was heating up. She leaned in closer. He smelled like woodsy aftershave with a hint of mint, ringing all of her pheromone bells. "How about you?"

He touched a lock of her hair. "Red and sweet."

If that wasn't an invitation, then she didn't know what was. This night was turning out miraculously better than a naked bubble bath.

Something behind her stole his attention. Alaina whirled around to the horror freak show that was her soprano rival, Bianca Pool.

"Look what the conductor dragged in." Bianca flung her bleached blonde hair over her shoulder. She wore a pink dress with an even lower neckline, revealing her assets to the point of a wardrobe malfunction. "Nice to see you again, Alaina."

"What are you doing here?" Alaina almost dropped her glass. "I thought you were in Germany."

"Altez offered me the Queen of the Night, and you know I can't turn that role up."

13

"You *are* very good at being wicked." Alaina tightened her grip on her glass. They'd be singing together. Ironically, the Queen of the night was her character's antagonist, and antagonize her, Bianca would.

Her rival stepped between her and Lance. "I came over to meet the famous Mr. DeBarr." She touched his arm. "I've heard a lot about you."

Lance shifted away from the two of them as if outnumbered. "What have you heard?"

"Only that you're the most successful stoke broker in New York. I read the article about you in Forbes last year. Your ideas for optimizing trading options are ingenious. Funny, the picture in the magazine didn't do you justice. You look even more gorgeous in real life."

"Thanks." He seemed more uncomfortable than impressed by her flattery. What a modest guy.

Alaina opened her mouth to compliment him on his modesty when Bianca angled her body in front of her and put her hand on his chest. "I want you to know I'm going to do everything it takes to be your highest bidder."

Alaina gagged silently.

"You are?" Was that fear or excitement flashing through his eyes? She tapped her purse. "I love donating to people in need."

Like hell she did. Bianca was more likely to kick a homeless man out of her way. Not that Alaina was much better, walking by them and pretending they weren't there.

Frustration built inside Alaina like a volcano heating up. Bianca had butted her out of the conversation. To make matters worse, Altez came over with Mrs. DeBarr on his arm. "Here she is; our new talent. Alaina, I'd like you to meet Mrs. DeBarr."

Alaina turned and shook her hand. "The pleasure is mine." Beside her, Bianca had entwined her arm in Lance's and turned him around toward the appetizers.

Damn it!

Alaina stifled a current of jealousy. Bianca may have won round one, but one thing was for sure. She wasn't letting that harlot win the bid.

***

As Brett talked to the blonde Barbie princess in front of him, he realized how little he knew about the stock market. The more he opened his mouth, the more he risked being found out for the poser that he was.

"What do you suggest I invest in this month?" She twirled the strap of her purse around her fingers. Even her nails were pink.

"With the market the way it is, it's hard to tell." Brett glanced around the room, distracted. Where was Alaina? When he'd first seen her at the party, he couldn't believe his eyes. The woman from the curb had been staring at *him* with interest. He had to remind himself she thought he was a billion dollars richer.

When he'd talked to her, their chemistry heated the room. He couldn't deny the way his body pulled toward her, aching to touch her sunset hair. She smelled like roses and lavender, reminding him of the meadow beyond the log cabin.

Even if he had to assume someone's identity to meet her, the embarrassment was totally worth it.

Mrs. DeBarr clinked her spoon on her glass, muting everyone's conversation. Brett turned toward the older woman with relief. The less he said tonight, the better, if he was ever going to get out of this alive.

"I want to thank you all for coming. Your generosity will bring happiness to those in need and support this wonderful opera in the process. Let's see this partnership of Project Wish and the Metropolitan Opera Fund flourish, and let's have some fun in the process. We begin tonight with our first annual auction."

As the crowd applauded, nervous jitters spiraled through him. He wasn't used to being the center of attention, never mind the grand prize of a million dollar auction. He had to remind himself this was for a charity he believed in, a charity he probably needed himself.

But, Brett would never take handouts. If he had to work extra hours to rebuild his life, so be it.

A man with white hair which stuck up like weeds introduced himself as Altez Vior and escorted Brett to a backroom. He was supposed to sit and wait for his turn while they started with smaller prizes like vintage wine and chocolate.

Hopefully one of those older ladies would outbid Ms. Barbie. He didn't want to talk about stock portfolios all night long. In any case, he'd have to do some homework on the real Lance DeBarr before this so called date.

The door opened, and Mrs. DeBarr snuck in. "How's my adopted son?"

"A little nervous." He'd lied so many times already; he figured he'd be honest with something. "Why couldn't I just be myself?"

She took a seat beside him and adjusted her velvet scarf. "Sadly enough, no one is going to pay thousands of dollars to go out with a construction worker."

He smiled. She was probably right. He wouldn't want to pay to hang around with half the men at work. "I can't imagine why."

She laughed. "I'm sure you're a great bunch. Look at you- such a gentleman, helping me raise money for this good cause."

He shrugged. He still felt like a schmuck assuming her son's identity. "What if someone who knows your real son sees me tonight?"

She shook her head. "Don't worry. My son is rarely seen in public. He keeps to himself and travels the world half the time. I see him maybe once a year. Besides, you do look kind of like him, plus a few pounds of muscle."

Did he pick up on a strain of melancholy in her voice? "Once a year?"

She nodded, tight lipped. All of a sudden she looked frail and vulnerable, her fancy velvet a façade for an aging, lonely woman. Brett took her hand. He was glad he'd come.

She placed her other hand over his and squeezed. "I'll have to thank your parents for allowing me to borrow you."

Brett sighed. How much should he tell her? "They're both gone."

She covered her heart with her hand. "Oh, I'm sorry. You're so young, I guess I thought…"

"They died before they should have."

Silence fell. His chest tightened, and no words would come. Brett wanted to tell her more, but he always closed up when anyone asked him about his family. It was as if talking about the fire made it more real. Better to live in denial, pretending his folks were still in the log cabin in Maine, his dad cutting firewood, and his mom stitching her embroidery pattern for the windowsills.

The door opened, and Altez poked his head in. "You're up next."

Brett jumped to his feet. Nervous energy coursed through him like that night a few years ago at the talent show in college, when he had stood backstage with his guitar. Only this was worse. They weren't judging him; they were *buying* him.

He followed Mrs. DeBarr and Altez onto the stage. Bright lights shone down, blacking out the audience for a second as his eyes adjusted. Most of the front and center seats were filled, everyone holding their numbered paddles. Ms. Barbie sat in the front row.

His pulse quickened.

He scanned the audience, but he couldn't find Alaina. She probably wasn't even bidding.

Altez took the podium. "The next item up for bid is the hand-some Mr. DeBarr, and one luxurious night out for two. Bidding starts at one thousand."

Brett almost choked. One thousand? Dollars?

Five paddles went up- four older ladies and Barbie's.

Altez raised both eyebrows as if impressed. "Do I hear two thousand?"

Come on older ladies. Hold your ground.

They all held up their paddles.

"Three thousand?"

Everyone was still in.

His collar tightened around his neck as Altez raised the bid as high as ten thousand. Three of the older women dropped out, leaving one older lady with blue-gray hair and Barbie.

The thought of disappointing the blonde princess weighed heavily on his shoulders. He was no stockbroker. He couldn't help her with her finances any more than he could wear her pink dress. If she knew who he really was, she'd be disgusted.

"I'll raise the bid to fifteen thousand." A voice called from the back.

Brett shielded his eyes against the light. Alaina stood from her seat, raising her bidding paddle over her head. Where did she come from? And why was she after him?

What did it matter? Somehow, he believed what had sparked between him and Alaina transcended any social barriers. He could feel her draw to him deep within his gut.

Or maybe he was just crazy and didn't want to go out with a pink nightmare.

The last older lady dropped out, leaving Barbie. She turned and sneered at Alaina. Then she held up her sign. "Sixteen thousand."

Alaina didn't blink an eye. "Twenty."

The audience collectively gasped. Barbie's face grew red and a vein at her temple pulsed as she slowly brought down her paddle.

Altez scanned the audience. "Twenty thousand going once, going twice...sold to Alaina Amaldi."

As the crowd clapped, Brett walked off stage in a daze. He was going on a date with Alaina Amaldi, the unattainable vision of beauty he'd seen from the street only hours before. And she'd paid for it. In big bucks.

Had he died and gone to heaven?

Trying not to burst his own bubble, he reminded himself, again, that she thought he was Lance DeBarr, sole inheritor to the DeBarr fortune. Did his status really matter to her?

Brett plopped in his seat as Altez and Mrs. DeBarr came in and congratulated him for attaining the biggest donation of the night. Seeing Mrs. DeBarr happy made posing as her son worth every risk.

He brought Mrs. DeBarr aside. "What do you know about Alaina Amaldi?"

Mrs. DeBarr looked away as if she was afraid to tell him the truth. "Only that she's the biggest diva who ever walked the stage of the Met."

"Great." He refused to believe her. The woman he'd met in the cocktail room had seemed like a lot of fun. Brett peered out the curtains to the audience. He was going to find out just what Alaina was looking for one way or the other.

CHAPTER THREE

Prize

Alaina leaned back in her seat in the audience, trying not to look too smug. Twenty thousand was like pennies to her. Thanks to the accounts her parents had set up for her future, she made more in interest every month.

Besides, it was for charity.

And anything was worth beating Bianca, no matter the cost. Not to mention she had the man of her choice, Lance DeBarr.

The auction ended with a few closing remarks. Afterwards, the audience mingled, congratulating each other on their winning bids. Alaina felt like queen of the universe as she cut through the crowd towards the backstage. She wanted to catch Lance before he left so they could solidify their plans.

A sly voice stopped her in her tracks.

"Just because you can buy your men doesn't mean you'll be able to buy your tenure here at the Met." Bianca crumpled her auction number underneath her pink nails. Some people were just sore losers.

Alaina stifled the rising current of anger. So what if she had to buy a date? Bianca would have done the same thing. If she could have afforded it. "What do you care? Don't you have a contract with some opera in Germany?"

"For now. But who knows what the future will bring, and I'm telling you, this place isn't big enough for both our voices."

Bianca and Alaina had been competing with each other ever since their Julliard days. She'd always claimed Alaina had bought her way into the school, while Bianca was there on scholarship. Maybe Alaina's parents had the money to send her there, but that didn't take away from the fact she was just as talented. You can buy a grand piano, but you couldn't buy a world-class voice.

Right now, Alaina wished Bianca could buy some tact. "They'll have to expand the stage, because I'm not going anywhere."

She pushed by Bianca and slipped backstage.

Lance sat in a chair resting his hand in his hand, exhaustion clear in his slumped shoulders. Maybe he had a long day at work? Who knew all the numbers he had to crunch and all the graphs he had to interpret? Math always made her head spin, and she had no interest in the stock market, but she couldn't deny her attraction to him.

Alaina took the seat beside him. "Long day?"

He glanced up and blinked in surprise. "You could say that."

"I know what that's like. I was supposed to be soaking in my bubble bath right about now."

His eyes flicked over her dress as if he imagined her in the tub.

Alaina smiled and crossed her legs. She wished they were both there right now.

"Thanks, by the way." His gaze delved deep into her eyes, making her blush.

"For what?"

"For saving my butt back there."

Butt? For a New York stockbroker, he talked like an ordinary guy. He was so laid back. Alaina was always wound up, and his natural calm soothed her. "How?"

"From that woman in pink."

Wow. He just shot up from hot to perfect in her eyes. Alaina played coy. "You mean you don't like her?"

"She's beautiful, don't get me wrong. And I'm sure she's great company. But, I didn't want to listen to her asking about stock portfolios all night."

Alaina laughed. Seems like Bianca tried too hard. "Well, you're in luck, because I have absolutely no interest whatsoever in the stock market."

He breathed with relief. "Then, I think we're going to have a great time."

Alaina shook her head, not knowing what to make of him. He was such a contradiction, wealthy yet modest, confident yet hesitant, sexy yet boyishly cute. Unlike most men, she couldn't read what was on his mind, although she suspected she was in there, somewhere.

"So, when is this date going to be?" She used her conversational, ambivalent tone, trying not to sound too eager.

He shrugged. "Whenever you want. My shifts usually end around seven."

"Shifts?"

"I mean, sometimes I work late at the…office."

"Oh." She hoped he wasn't a workaholic. Gotta have time for those bubble baths.

He drummed his finger on the armrest of his chair. "So when are you free?"

"Let me see…" She was supposed to volunteer at Heart House tomorrow until three, and rehearsals didn't start until the following night. "How about tomorrow night?"

"Sounds good."

"How dressy should I be?"

He gave her a suggestive smile. "What you're wearing now is nice."

Boy did she like this guy. Alaina teased him with a little slap on the arm. "I can't wear the same outfit two days in a row!"

22

His dark eyes sparkled. "I don't mind."

"I'll find something similar." Her mind went through every outfit she'd ever owned. Better raid the closet when she got home. "And where are we going?"

He raised both eyebrows. "That's a secret."

Alaina nodded. "Of course. You like keeping secrets?"

His face darkened. "No. As a matter of fact I don't. But, this has to be special. You paid twenty thousand dollars after all."

Good. Because she'd been burned by secrets before- like when her roommate on her Italian tour stole her guy. She'd brought herself to forgive her, but still, secrets were never good. "I'm sure you'll make it worthwhile."

"I'll certainly try."

"So you'll pick me up?"

"Eight o'clock. I can pick you up here, or at your place. It's up to you."

She figured he was safe. He was Mrs. DeBarr's son after all. Everyone in the entire fundraiser knew they were going out. "My place. Paramount Tower – 240 East 39th Street. I'll be in the lobby."

His gaze widened as though he was impressed. Sure it was a nice place to live, but she bet he had her beat. Not that she liked him for his money. She was so well off, Alaina didn't need a guy with money. The last guy she fell for was an Italian tour guide. And she could guess how much he made.

What mattered was their chemistry, and with this guy, they were way off the charts.

***

Brett collapsed onto the orange plaid couch he'd found by the garbage dumpster. He wished he had something with access to the internet. Where the hell was he going to take someone who'd just paid for a twenty thousand dollar date?

Mrs. DeBarr gave him a limitless credit card and told him he could buy whatever it took, but she didn't give him any advice on *what* to buy. Sure, he could take Alaina to some fancy restaurant downtown, but he wanted to show her a little of who he was and what he liked. Only then would he be able to discern if it was worth sticking around and telling her the truth.

If he decided to pursue a relationship, then ultimately he would have to tell her. And not just about his vocation. He'd have to tell her about the fire, open up like he hadn't been able to do in the past.

Brett walked to the fridge and opened a beer. He was getting ahead of himself. He had to play it one day at a time. She may not even like the same things he did. Heck, she was an opera star and he was a logger from Maine. What could they possibly have in common?

For now, all he had to worry about was which restaurant to choose and getting to bed on time for an early shift tomorrow. He couldn't be caught snoozing on a fancy china plate at dinner.

He took a sip, trying to calm himself. He had the whole day tomorrow to come up with something. Maybe some of the guys had an idea.

He thought of Phil's comment about the flagpole up her ass. *Now I know I'm getting tired.*

Phil would probably tell him to go out for beer and chicken wings.

Which wasn't far from what he was used to. But, he had to find some middle ground. No caviar. But also, sadly, no chicken wings.

Up in Maine, he used to go to a family owned steakhouse. It was a nice sit-down restaurant renovated from an old train station. The old wooden pillars gave the dining room a rugged, rustic feel of Maine. He loved it.

Maybe he could find something like that here in New York?

Brett threw his bottle in the recycling bin.

Tomorrow he'd get Phil to go on his fancy iPhone and do a search. He'd find a nice restaurant which also challenged her cultural perceptions. Her reaction would give him the information he needed. She might hate it and he might crash and burn. But, he wasn't willing to open his heart to just any woman. Failure was worth the price for the truth.

CHAPTER FOUR

Opera Witch

The alarm blared in Alaina's ears. She stuffed her head under her pillow and moaned. How could anyone get up at this ungodly hour?

Most of the world did. Teachers, nurses, TV anchors, bakers, businessmen like Lance. If they could do it, she could.

Slamming her hand on the alarm, she pulled herself out of bed. If she wanted that role, then she'd better get her butt in gear. Alaina threw herself in a scalding hot shower to wake herself up. The last time she'd gotten up this early was back in her Julliard days for music theory, and she hadn't always made it on time. Or at all.

Now more than a grade rested on the line.

She slipped on a pair of navy pants and a blouse and twisted her hair in a bun, to make her best teacher impression. At least she looked the part.

So maybe she'd never taught anyone in her life, or talked with high school kids. She could act like no tomorrow, and act she would.

She hailed a cab and rode to the crummy part of the Bronx, where she wouldn't be caught dead walking alone at night. Or more like, she would be dead if she did. She paid the cab driver extra to pull up right to the door, then grabbed her purse and entered the building feeling like it was *her* first day of school all over again.

An older, worn out looking woman in the office told her she'd be subbing for a teacher on maternity leave and directed her to room three fifteen.

Her heels clicked on the linoleum as she paced quickly to the room. Her school had polished floors, brand new lockers, and reproductions of Monet's works hanging on the wall. This school had scuffed floors, beaten in lockers with graffiti scrawled in all manner of curses, and bare walls. Her heat raced, and her throat constricted. If she'd tried to sing anything, it would have come out as a cracked whisper.

When she opened the door, a girl with purple hair sat on her desk picking at holes in her racy stockings, while a guy dressed in black with black eyeliner played Candy Crush on his phone. Three other hoodlums with saggy pants and baseball hats pulled sideways over greasy hair wrote profanities on the chalkboard. None of them even looked up at her entrance.

Alaina clutched her purse tightly to her chest and walked to the front of class. "Good morning students. My name is Alaina Amaldi, and I'll be taking the place of your teacher today."

They didn't look impressed. Alaina was used to getting standing ovations, and these students barely stayed awake or made eye contact. She had an urge to tell them just who the hell she was, but somehow she didn't think that would impress them either.

"Take your seats and shut off your phones." She gave the goth guy a steady glare. The previous teacher had left her a book on the desk, and she opened it to a page with a substitute lesson plan on Bach.

Thank god. She'd sung enough Bach to teach a whole semester.

"Take out your books and turn to page twenty seven."

Three kids dug into grimy backpacks, while the rest of them just sat there.

"I said, take out your books."

A gangly boy hiding half his face under his hood raised his hand. "I don't have a book." The rest of the class laughed.

Alaina started erasing the profanity on the chalkboard. "Share with someone next to you."

When she turned around, half the class still didn't have a book. She glanced at the girl with the purple hair. "And where's your book?"

The girl gave her an I-don't-give-a-shit kind of look. "I left mind at home."

"O-kay." Alaina resisted the urge to roll her eyes. "No matter. I'll read the chapter out loud." She cleared her voice. "Bach was a German composer, organist, harpsichordist, violist and violinist of the Baroque Period." She glanced up. "Now, who can tell me when the Baroque period was?"

Purple hair raised her hand. "Can't we study some great music legend of today, like Justin Bieber?"

The whole class burst out laughing. Alaina closed the book. Looks like the traditional method wasn't working. At all. "I happen to like Bach. I've sung many of his cantatas and oratorios. They are beautiful staples of vocal literature."

"What are you, some kind of opera witch?" A boy grumbled while writing on his desk.

Again, raucous laughter erupted.

Alaina fought a rising wave of panic. She wanted to run from the room and back to her safe apartment on the east side where people had manners. How dare they talk to her like this?

But, if she gave up, she'd be reinforcing exactly what the president of the board thought of her- a pampered rich socialite who wasn't capable of holding down a volunteer job, never mind expressing compassion or unrequited love.

She was stronger and smarter than that.

Maybe it was time to broaden her image. She couldn't let these little bullies defeat her. She needed them on her side. She needed to show them opera wasn't some stuffed up snobby thing of the past. It could actually be a lot of fun.

Think, Alaina think. "Opera witch" reminded her of Bianca and her role as the Queen of the Night. Then, an idea sparked in her mind.

As the laughter settled down, she straightened up, crossed her arms and addressed the student. "As a matter of fact, sometimes I am."

The students quieted. Some of the ones who'd been on their phones the whole time glanced up. She had their attention.

Alaina paced the front of the classroom, drumming her fingers on her elbows. "Opera is made up of stories. Sometimes you play the sweet heroine, and other times you play the evil villain." She raised an eyebrow. "Anyone know who Carmen is?"

Silence, then one hand went up. "You mean Carmen Electra?"

A few of them giggled.

Alaina shook her head. "Approximately one hundred and forty years before Carmen Electra, there was *the original* Carmen in an opera by Bizet. She was a seductress who enchanted a young soldier with exotic dances. His unbridled passion for her drove him to forsake his duty and the woman his mother wants him to marry. But Carmen is not a one type of guy kind of gal. She tires of the soldier and falls in love with another man. In the end, the soldier pleads for her to return to him. When she refuses, he stabs her, killing her on the spot."

"Or take Puccini's *Turandot*- a daughter of a Chinese empire who is looking for a husband. She asks each suitor three questions. If they answer correctly, she marries them, but if they fail…" She chopped her hand down on the front desk and the boy who sat in it jerked up.

Alaina smiled wickedly. "They lose their heads."

She took a tissue from the box on her desk and covered the bottom half of her face. "I've also studied the infamous Salome who enchants the head of the palace with her dance of the seven veils. He agrees to give her her heart's desire. But, little does he know her heart's desire is the head of a man who'd rejected her advances...on a plate."

"Ouch. Tough luck for him, huh?" Purple hair actually leaned forward across her desk, engaged with what she was saying.

"Maybe you'll think twice about scorning any admirers." Alaina winked. "Anyway, when Salome gets the head on the plate, what do you think she does with it?"

"She kicks it." Purple hair crossed her arms. "That's what I would do."

"No, I bet she sticks it on a pole to show everyone what happens when they piss her off." The boy without the book didn't raise his hand, but she let his comment go. At least he was involved in the conversation.

"Not quite." Alaina gave them a mysterious smile. "She kissed it."

"Ewwww." Purple hair scrunched up her pretty little nose pierced by several nose rings.

Alaina went on to tell them stories of all the characters she'd played or studied in the past. Before she knew it, the bell rang, and they students stood from their seats.

"Wait a second!" Alaina held them in their places by the commanding tone of her voice. She'd grown more and more confident as the class went on. "For your homework, I want you to start writing your very own opera."

"What? We can't do that." Goth guy whined like a baby.

"Yes you can. You're all students here at this arts school. You've all taken theory and writing classes. You have a mind- an imagination."

Goth boy opened his mouth to complain again and she cut him off by raising her hand. "Don't worry I'll help you through it, step by step. Tonight I want you to think of a setting for your story. That's all. Just a place."

As the students filed out, Purple hair approached her desk. "See you tomorrow, right?"

"That's right." Alaina sipped from her water bottle, expecting the student to walk away. But she didn't move. "Is there something else?"

"No. I'm Jackie, by the way." She stuck her hands in her pockets.

Alaina nodded and made a mental note to remember her name. She didn't know any of their names and if she was in this for the long haul, then she should learn them. "Nice to meet you."

"I sing, too. I don't have a teacher or anything, but I like to harmonize to songs on the radio."

Alaina blinked in surprise. "I'll have to hear you sing sometime."

"I'd like that." Jackie picked up her backpack and left.

Alaina watched the girl turn the corner. At the beginning of class, she could have cared less about Alaina, and now here she was staying late to tell her she sang, too. Alaina smiled to herself as she packed up her purse.

There was hope after all. For both of them.

***

"Why do you want me to look up a fancy restaurant?" Phil stuffed the rest of his tuna sandwich in his mouth.

Brett threw the other half of his ham sandwich back in the bag. The bread was stale and he wasn't hungry anyway.

"Well?" Phil took out his phone and turned it on. "We only have five more minutes of break."

Brett crumpled the bag and stuffed it under his feet. He wasn't going to get his friend's help unless he told him the truth. "Because I have a date."

"A date?" Phil widened his eyes. "Looks like it didn't take you long to get over that red head from yesterday."

Brett ran his hand over his face. Was asking Phil a mistake? "It *is* the red head from yesterday."

He spit out his soda. "What? How'd you manage that?"

"It's a long story. Now, can you help me or not?"

Phil wiped his mouth on his sleeve and pulled out his iPhone. "Sure. What exactly do you want me to look up?"

"I want to take her to someplace nice, but also someplace that reflects who I am. I don't want her believing me to be someone I'm not." Brett ran his hands though his hair.

A little too late for that, isn't it?

Phil nodded. "I get ya. Sarah was always trying to dress me up and get me to go to all these weird art exhibits. It all just looked like splattered paint to me."

Oh no, not Sarah again. Phil could talk about the-one-that-got-away for hours.

Phil stared into the traffic. "Maybe I should have just gone with her and stopped complaining."

"You were just being yourself."

"Yeah, but it wasn't *that* bad. Man, what I wouldn't give to have another chance. I'd go to every museum in New York, even that American folk art museum. You know once they had an entire exhibit of quilts. Quilts."

Brett tightened his lips to keep from smiling. Quilts weren't exactly high on his priority list, either. "I get your point."

Phil went back to his phone. "So what do you want me to look for?"

Brett told him about the restaurant up in Maine. He hadn't mentioned Maine other than to tell people that was where he was from. Speaking of his hometown made me feel vulnerable, naked. "Can you search for something like that around here?"

"I'll try." Phil dragged his finger across the screen. "What about this?"

Brett glanced at a picture of a restaurant on a rooftop with a garden overlooking the city. "Kinda, but it's not very secluded."

"You want secluded? In New York?" Phil laughed. "How about this?"

A picture of a Moosehead beer on top of a bar came up. Brett shook his head. "Not nice enough."

"Geez, aren't you Mr. Picky?"

Brett stood. "Look, I'm sorry I bothered you."

"No, no, no. It's no bother. It's just what you're looking for doesn't exist." Phil shut off his phone and stuffed it back in the pocket of his jeans. "Too bad you can't rent a jet and fly her there."

Wait a second. Mrs. DeBarr had said to do whatever it took. Brett pointed at Phil. "That's not a bad idea."

Phil stood and they stared walking back to the construction site. "I was joking, man. Where you gonna get the money for something like that?"

Brett clapped his friend on the shoulder feeling more confident than ever. This would be a night she'd remember. "Leave that to me."

CHAPTER FIVE

Looking Too Hard

Alaina paced the front of the lobby in her black heels. She'd found a dress like the one she'd worn last night, with a little more glamor. This one was black with a solid top and a lacy underskirt revealing her legs from her ankles to her upper thighs, with a mini dress underneath. It was elegant enough for a formal dinner with a subtle sexuality.

I hope he likes it.

She'd forgotten to ask what his car looked like. She could tell a lot about a man from the car he chose to drive, and she wanted to know more about Lance DeBarr. A lot more. There was something so different about him- a cool modesty and a relaxed simplicity that the other guys she met didn't have. He wasn't trying to prove himself to anyone. If anything, he was trying to blend in. She could learn from him. She shouldn't always have to be the center of attention. Life would be much easier for her if she could learn to step aside.

Maybe then Bianca wouldn't bother her as much.

A black limo pulled up to the curb. Anxious nerves climbed up her arms and legs. Was this for her? As much as she wanted to see *his* car, she never passed up a chance to ride in style.

Lance stepped out dressed in a crisp, white button down shirt and black slacks, looking laid back, yet classic. His dark brown hair fell in natural waves around his ears, and she longed to run her hands through it. Alaina took a deep breath and stepped through the revolving door.

The September air hit her like a brisk slap, and she wished she'd brought her fur coat instead of the little black leather one. But this one matched her dress better- and fashion came first. Especially on a first date. Later on down the line she could start bringing out the comfy clothes.

Lance's face softened into a fond smile when he saw her, making her feel like they were best friends from way back. "Hi, Alaina."

"Hey."

His gaze glanced over her dress. The lace fluttered in the wind, and his eyes settled on the short underskirt. "I like that one, too."

"I thought you would." Any guy who complimented her on her clothes won extra points in her book. It showed he cared enough to notice details.

He opened the door for her and offered his hand to help her in. She slid her fingers in his, feeling the rough calluses and the warmth of his touch. She didn't want to let go.

Alaina slid into her seat. Lance closed the door behind her and circled the limo. He said something to the driver, but she couldn't make out any words.

The door on the other side opened, and he sat in the passenger seat behind the driver.

She adjusted her lacey skirt. "So where are we going?"

Lance shook his head and "tsked tsked" as though she'd been naughty. "Still a surprise."

The driver took off, and Alaina wished she knew something about the evening he'd planned. She pouted her lower lip. "Can't you give me a clue?"

Lance crossed his arms and scrunched his mouth to the side,

like he was thinking really hard. "Hmm…it's got something to do with trees."

"Trees?" There weren't that many trees in New York. "We're not going to Central Park are we?"

He laughed. "No."

"Good."

His features turned vulnerable. "What's wrong? You don't like the outdoors?"

Did she like the outdoors? She'd never really thought of it before. "To tell you the truth, I haven't spent much time outdoors. I grew up in this city and went to school at Julliard. Most of my time was spent studying and performing inside concert halls and practice rooms."

He furrowed his brow. "Have you ever gone hiking?"

"Nope."

"Canoeing?"

"Nope."

"Camping?"

She shook her head. "Definitely not."

"Wow." He sat back stunned. An awkward silence fell between them.

Alaina played with her seatbelt, wondering if she'd already ruined their date. Was the outdoors so important to him? Maybe it was like someone telling her they'd never heard opera? She'd probably discount them like they were some type of fool. But was that the right thing to do? Would she want Lance to discount her just because she never held a canoe paddle?

Opera was the center of her life. But did it define her, or was she more than a beautiful voice? "Why do people go camping anyway?"

Lance laughed like he didn't believe she'd just asked that. "The outdoors can be very relaxing. For me, it's a kind of release, like breathing deeply after holding my breath for too long. It clears my mind and helps me sort things out."

Her mind did feel cluttered at times from the traffic, the smog, and the perpetual noise of the city. Maybe she'd been missing out all these years? Alaina reached out and touched his hand. "Just because I haven't had the experience, doesn't mean I don't want to try."

Hope glimmered in his eyes. "You sure?"

"Yeah." She meant it. Maybe she'd been too narrow minded, always thinking about her concerts and her practicing. "I've been focused on my career since I was five and my parents started taking me to auditions. I guess I've never had the time to explore other hobbies."

He ran his fingers over hers and threaded heir hand together. "Do you have the time for me?"

Alaina didn't hesitate. "I'll make the time." Once she said it out loud, she realized she had no other choice. She'd regret this for the rest of her life if she didn't explore what she had with this man.

He relaxed his shoulders and smiled. "Good, because I think you're missing out."

Alaina glanced out the window. The limo had pulled into the back of the airport and parked next to a hanger. Her jaw dropped.

"No way. We're not going on a plane, are we?"

He nodded and got out of the car. "A Pilatus to be exact."

Alaina followed him into the hanger, where two pilots waited by a sleek, white jet. They shook Lance's hand and helped them up the stairs. Eight leather seats stretched out across the back of the plane. Lance must have ordered champagne, because a bottle waited for them on a small pull out table. He opened it up and poured two glasses as Alaina took her seat.

"I thought this would help with the jitters." He handed her a glass and sat beside her.

"Don't worry. I fly all the time." Alaina took the glass and sipped. Even though she did fly around the world- heck she'd gone to Italy last summer, her nerves were acting up. Was it the excitement of the trip or because she was there with Lance?

He took a large gulp of his champagne. Maybe she wasn't the only one with nerves.

"Do you? So where does a beautiful and famous soprano like you go?"

She blushed. He just called her beautiful. "Oh you know. Here and there. Sometimes I fly out for an audition or a guest performance."

His dark eyes turned dreamy, as if he imagined her life. "Where is the most special place you've ever sung?"

"The most special? Gosh, I have to think about that." Most men asked her about how much she made, who she'd sung for, or what famous people she'd sung with. But not Lance. He didn't care about name-dropping or money, only about what she liked.

"I guess it would have to be the vineyard I'd sung at last summer on my Italian tour."

"What made it so special?"

"I sang well, for one." In fact, it was that very performance that got her the newspaper quote that propelled her career. "But, it was more than that. There was something magical about the call of the birds in the background and the smell of the flowers. It was probably why I sang so well. I was inspired by the timeless atmosphere."

His traced a line over her hand and up her arm, which sent shivers through her body. "Maybe you really do like the outdoors, and you just don't know it yet."

"Maybe I do."

The plane took off, and Alaina gripped her seat. "How long is this trip?"

"A little under an hour. Don't worry, I'll get you home before curfew."

She laughed. "I guess I do have a curfew now."

"Why's that?"

"I'm volunteering at a local charter school for the arts. They start classes at eight am sharp."

"I had no idea you were so kind hearted."

Alaina glanced down, unable to hold his gaze. Should she tell him the truth? It was embarrassing, but she didn't want to keep anything from him. Somehow, she thought he'd understand. If he didn't then he wouldn't like her anyway and this whole night was for naught. He had to know her, warts and all. She'd lost the Italian guy because she tried too hard to impress him with all her accomplishments. All that she had done was to push him away-right into her roommate's arms.

Alaina breathed deeply. "I'm not. To tell you the truth, I've never volunteered in my life. I just never thought about it."

He stared right into her eyes as if seeing her soul. "So why are you doing it now?"

"The board of directors of the opera put me up to it. I'm supposed to be cleaning up my image."

He blinked as though surprised, then curled the right side of his lips. "Are you a late night party girl?"

Alaina slapped her hand on her forehead. "My god, no! It's not that." Her tone grew serious. "They don't think I'm capable of the sweet unrequited love my character has to portray."

He touched her hair near her ear, smoothing it down and studied her as if she was the most intriguing beauty he'd ever seen. "Are you?"

Staring into his gorgeous brown eyes, Alaina sure hoped so. "I'm not sure if I've ever been in true love before. It's never seemed to last."

"That's because you haven't found the right man." His smile seemed to suggest the right man sat right next to her. Or maybe it was all her imagination.

Alaina traced a circle on the back of his palm. "And you're an expert in such things?"

"Not an expert." Lance glanced at his champagne, suddenly boyishly embarrassed. "Just an observer."

Lance was so good at asking questions, Alaina had been talking the whole time about herself. She hadn't learned any more about him. "What have you observed?"

He shrugged. "Love can hit you when you least expect it, but it never comes when you're looking too hard."

Alaina thought about how she'd pushed her relationship with the Italian guy. She'd wanted love so badly on that trip. Maybe it was because she was singing about a wedding, or because she hadn't been in a relationship for a long time. Or it could have been the romantic Italian countryside. Whatever it was, by forcing it, she'd driven love away. "You're right."

The plane landed, and they stepped out into cool, misty air. Thick, tall pine trees surrounded a small, hole-in-the-wall airport with one landing strip and a run-down cabin posing as the welcome center.

Alaina hugged her shoulders against the chill night. "Where are we?"

Lance put his arm around her. "Northern Maine." Pride surged in his voice.

"Maine?" She'd never been to Maine. She'd never had a reason to. Panic shot up her spine as she glanced at the pine trees stretching to the sky. She had a sudden urge to get back on the plane. "There are bathrooms where we're going, right?"

He laughed. "Yes, very nice ones."

"Thank goodness." He had her scared for a minute there. He hugged her close. "Trust me. I know you don't have much experience with the outdoors, so I'm introducing you in small steps."

Did she trust him? She'd bought a twenty thousand dollar date, gotten into a dark limo, and onto a private jet. So yeah, she must've trusted him at least a little. "Okay."

Another limo appeared from the empty road as if on command. Lance stepped toward it and opened the door. "After you."

Alaina got in and sat down. What was in Maine anyway? George Bush Senior had a house on the coast, but she doubted they were visiting him. Lobsters and lighthouses; she knew Maine was famous for that. But not northern Maine. They must be miles from the coast.

The only other thing that came to mind was all those horror novels that took place in Maine. She grabbed Lance's arm. "Tell me we're not visiting Stephen King."

He laughed. "No, we're not."

The limo drove through hilly streets with trees on either side and climbed a ridge, pulling up to a log cabin lit with golden light that overlooked the valley below. A sign hung on a carved tree beside the glass doorway which read *Twilight Woods Inn and Resort*.

Alaina stepped out and took Lance's arm. Below them, the forest stretched for miles. Being so far from the city in a secluded area scared her. But, it was also freeing in a way she'd never felt before. "This is gorgeous."

He placed his hand on top of hers. "I hoped you'd like it."

They walked through the glass doors and into the main lobby. Everything was wood; the floor, the beams, the furniture, the stairs. It was like the whole place was carved from a giant piece of oak. At the center, a massive stone fireplace glowed with flames. It reminded Alaina of a time long past, when people sat by a fire and sipped cocoa instead of watching TV.

The lodging was off to the right, a spa branched to the left, and at the center, up the grand stairway the dining room bustled with activity.

Lance practically glowed as he led her up the stairs. His natural ease with the place made Alaina wonder if he'd been coming here for a long time. If so, he'd shared a special place that meant something to him, which warmed her heart.

A hostess greeted them with a big smile, then sat them down by a large window overlooking the valley. A crescent moon hung high above them and the vast forest stretched in all directions.

Alaina unfolded her napkin. "This is truly unique. Thank you for taking me here." An actual social life existed outside New York- and one that she wanted to be a part of.

He leaned back in his seat and breathed with relief as he laid his eyes on the forest. "My pleasure."

41

"Of all the places in the north east, why Maine? Why this place?"

Lance glanced around the room. "I grew up around here."

"You did?" She couldn't picture Mrs. DeBarr hiking in the woods. "A summer home?"

Lance coughed and reached for the water. He took a long sip. "Of course. Yes, a summer home."

"It must be beautiful. I'd like to see it."

His gaze trailed off across the room. "It was."

She froze with her glass halfway to her mouth. "Was?"

He shifted uncomfortably in his chair. "It was destroyed by a fire."

Alaina's chest tightened. The pain in his eyes cut right to her core. She reached across the table and took his hand. "Oh that's horrible. I'm so sorry."

He waved her concerns away. "I don't want to spoil this night talking about the past."

"Of course." Guilt rolled over her for bringing such a painful subject up. And on a first date no less. Geez, she was striking out all over the place with her apparent inexperience with the wilderness, her sob story about her volunteering and now this. "I keep saying the wrong thing."

"No. It's not you." He squeezed her hand. "You've been wonderful. You're the reason why I had to confidence to come back."

Alaina covered her heart with her hand. "You mean you haven't been back since?"

He shook his head and gave her a look that would melt hearts. "I had to show you something special."

Alaina covered her mouth, overwhelmed. "My goodness. I don't know what to say."

He laced his fingers through hers. "Don't say anything. Just be here with me."

CHAPTER SIX

Heroes and Villains

Brett had no idea that coming back would hit him so hard. The smell of the fresh pine brought a roaring wave of melancholy, making him wonder why he'd left. A sharp ache in his gut told him he'd had no other choice.

He hadn't thought of the consequences of returning, only that he wanted Alaina to experience a taste of home with him. Having her there grounded him, made him feel like there was a future in New York, that the fire hadn't eaten his soul. That he *could* come back.

Boy, was he glad she'd come.

He ordered his favorite, the grilled steak with fries, and she ordered the chicken breast in a brandy mushroom cream sauce.

"This is delicious." Alaina took another bite, and Brett watched the fork leave her soft, red lips- lips he wanted to kiss.

Alaina brushed her sunset hair over her shoulder. "Who would have known this wonderful place existed in the middle of nowhere?"

"Only the locals." Brett smiled with pride. "They keep it that way for a reason."

Alaina raised an eyebrow. "To keep rude New Yorkers like me out?"

Brett laughed. He loved her sassy sense of humor. "To keep it quaint."

He felt something brush his leg under the table. Alaina smiled and took another bite. One thing he learned about her- she wasn't shy. She knew what she wanted and she went after it. He'd never dated a girl who was so aggressive before. Usually they turned him off. But after the fire, he needed a good push in the right direction. He needed Alaina.

Brett reminded himself not to get too attached. She thought he was some rich businessman named Lance. When his cover fell, she may not like what was left.

"Do you always date wealthy businessmen?" He kept his tone trivial.

"Not at all." Alaina sipped her wine. "You're the first."

Then who was her type? Brett took another bite. "Do you ever date average Joes, you know, like normal, everyday people?"

She shook her finger at him. "You're hardly an average Joe."

A wave of frustration came over him. He wasn't getting anywhere with this. "You'd be surprised."

Alaina spread her hands. "This restaurant is far from normal in my estimation."

Brett laughed at the irony of her comment. "It's normal for me."

Alaina narrowed her eyes. "Do you ever date opera singers?"

Brett resisted the urge to roll his eyes. That's what he got for asking weird questions. A little of his own medicine. "No. But my first girlfriend in high school played the clarinet."

"Oh really?" Alaina tapped her napkin over her red lips. "You're making me jealous."

He couldn't tell if she was serious. His first girlfriend also had braces and pigtails. "You have nothing to be jealous about."

"Good. Because I want you all for myself."

Desire surged inside him. He loved how forward she was.

44

Forget all that insecure dating nonsense. Alaina got right down to business.

"And you shall."

After dinner, Brett led her around the back of the hotel. The full moon shone clear and bright, lighting their path.

"I hope there aren't any bears or bobcats in those woods." Alaina picked her way through the rocky path in her heels.

"Trust me, I've walked this way my whole life and I've never run into them. It's too close to civilization. You'd be surprised, sometimes they're more afraid of us than we are of them." She really didn't know much about the woods. Could she really be happy with someone like him?

"What the-" She jerked her hand over her arm and brushed violently at her sleeve.

He stopped and pulled her aside. "Are you okay?"

She ran her hand through her hair, her eyes wide and her movements finicky. "It must have been a bug."

"It's okay." He took her hand, trying to calm her. "I don't like bugs myself, but you get used to them over time. They can't hurt you."

"If only they'd mind their own business." She lurched forward, stumbling on the uneven path. Before he could steady her, she slipped and fell against him, grabbing his arm. He caught her, holding her close. "Whoa! Are you all right?" The evening was falling apart.

She shivered, and he thought she was crying. *Oh Geez.* She'd never agree to go out with him again. Never mind 'special,' this date was a nightmare.

Alaina lifted her head, and her eyes sparkled as she broke out in laughter. "You must think I'm a complete idiot, walking out here with these heels on."

He breathed with relief. Maybe she wasn't used to the outdoors, but she was taking it all in stride. "I'm the idiot. I didn't tell you how to dress. You had no idea what to wear."

"It's okay." She squeezed his hand. "I like surprises and you certainly had me guessing."

At least she liked the surprise. Maybe the night wasn't falling to pieces. Would she give this outdoors thing one more chance? "It's just a little further, if you think you can manage?"

She patted his hand. "With you I can."

Her words melted the wall he'd built around his heart. He hadn't had anyone need him since the fire. To know she relied on him made him felt needed, wanted, necessary.

They walked over a wooden bridge on the other side of a gurgling stream. Brett picked up two stones, one for him and one for her. He handed her the rock and his fingers brushed against hers longingly.

This would tell the real truth about her. He'd never showed this place to anyone before, afraid they'd make fun of him. But, after such a wonderful dinner, he was determined to learn as much as he could. "When I was a boy, I used to blow on a rock, throw it in the water and make a wish."

Feeling a little hokey, he blew on his rock, closed his eyes and wished he could learn more about her. He threw the rock in, and turned to Alaina. "Your turn."

Her eyes widened and she held the rock like a sacred stone. "My goodness. I'm not sure what to wish for." The way she took his ritual so seriously convinced him she was a keeper.

He closed his hand over hers. "Wish for something you want to come true. But, don't tell me."

She smiled. "I won't."

He released her hand reluctantly. Alaina blew on her rock and threw it across the stream. It bounced on a tree and landed with a thump in the forest.

She covered her mouth with her hand. "Oh my."

Brett laughed at how genuinely distraught she was. "That's quite an arm you've got."

"Guess my wish doesn't come true."

"You know what?" He picked up another rock. "I never told you the rule about second chances."

She took the rock from his hands. "What about them?"

"Second chances guarantee the wish comes true."

***

They took the limo back to the plane. Brett wished he could spend longer with her in Maine, but they both had to be back for their jobs in the morning, and an overnight vacation was not part of the bid.

He wasn't sure what Mrs. DeBarr would think if he took Alaina on a romantic weekend getaway. He was supposed to be entertaining the buyer for a dinner date, not seducing them or taking advantage of Lance's high status to get lucky.

They settled into their seats as the plane took off. Alaina nuzzled her head onto his shoulder. "I don't want to go back. Not yet."

Brett breathed in the rosy scent of her hair, trying to savor the moment. He entangled his fingers in hers. "Me neither."

How long could he uphold this façade? Mrs. DeBarr would be asking for her credit card back, and he sure as hell couldn't afford to take Alaina anywhere on his construction worker's pay when he could barely afford to make rent.

An incredible urge to tell her the truth came over him like a fever. He bit his tongue, not wanting Mrs. DeBarr to get in trouble. They couldn't have Alaina asking for her money back. He didn't think she'd do such a thing, but he also didn't know her very well. The questions he'd asked during the date had helped to paint a picture of a sassy woman who knew what she wanted and went for it, someone who was trying to open her heart as well as advance her career. She was driven, daring, and sensual, and he loved everything about her.

But was she able to understand him for who he really was? To forgive the sparkly façade he'd put on for a good cause?

He couldn't risk telling her the truth. Not yet.

They arrived back in the hanger and took the limo to Alaina's apartment building. Alaina watched him across the limo seat. She unbuckled and slid over, sitting against him. Her leg brushed against his pants, igniting heat deep inside him. "Thank you for such a wonderful night."

"Even with the rocks and the bugs?"

"Especially with the rocks and the bugs- they made things interesting."

Interesting was right. At least they broke the ice between them, which made taking her hand all that more easy. "You're the one I should thank." He took her hand. "You saved me from a night of stock quotes."

Alaina laughed. "Anytime."

Anytime. Was that an invitation for a second date? Hope and despair surged in equal measure. He couldn't pull this off on a second date, yet he couldn't deny the hot chemistry between them. He had to see her again. "Are you asking me out again?"

"Looks like it." Alaina brushed her nose against his jawline, and he felt her soft, smooth skin. *Damn.* His body charged with energy and his lips gravitated towards hers. She closed the distance, and kissed him fiercely, playing with his lower lip with her tongue.

He kissed her back, probing her lips and entering her mouth. The kiss went deep into his soul, waking him as though he'd been in a long, listless sleep. His hands traveled the curves of her body, and he pulled against the seatbelt to get closer. She tasted like sweet wine and warm, lustful woman, and he wanted her so badly, he forgot who he was supposed to be. All he could think of was her and him and how they should be entwined together, naked in his bed.

The limo stopped, and Alaina jolted forward crashing into the front seat.

She laughed and he pulled her up. "Are you okay?"

She nodded, her cheeks flushed red. She looked so beautiful.

"That's what you get for not wearing a seatbelt."

The date was at an end. The world and all its cruel reality hit him like a punch in the gut. Brett unbuckled his seatbelt and opened the door, needing fresh air to cool him off. "I'll walk you to the door."

He rounded the limo and opened Alaina's door. She took his arm as they walked to the hotel. "You know, you could come up. Stay awhile."

The offer was so enticing, he had to hold his breath before he could trust himself to give her an answer. If he wasn't assuming someone else's identity. If this wasn't an auctioned date for charity. If Mrs. DeBarr wasn't involved…so many possibilities drove him wild. "We both have to work early."

"Of course." Alaina detached her arm. "Another time, then."

Oh he certainly hoped so.

She slid him her card. "My number's on the back. Or should I just attend the next auction?"

Brett laughed and took the card, slipping it into his pocket. "Hopefully, I'll never have to go on display again."

"All in the name of charity, right?"

"Of course."

"Call me. I'll be waiting." She blew him a kiss and disappeared into the building. Brett clenched and unclenched both fists and then ran both hands through his hair. It had taken all of his self-control to let her go. In her absence, his entire body ached. He reminded himself that his limo would turn into a pumpkin soon, and he' go back to drilling and hammering in the morning.

Best take the ride home now.

He slid back into the limo and took out her card. Her alluring face stared back at him along with a quote, 'entrancing tone and dramatic dynamic range.'

Written on the back in elegant penmanship was her number. Brett ran his hands over the writing wondering when the best time was to tell her the truth.

Six am came at Alaina in a wailing alarm that cut through her pleasant dreams. She slammed her hand on the button and buried her face in the pillow. It had taken her a while to fall asleep last night, considering she'd just had the best date of her life.

She sat up, rummaged through her purse and checked her cell phone. No calls. Of course, he wouldn't call in the middle of the night. She was being ridiculous. He'd probably wait a day or two, or maybe until the weekend, and then give her a ring. She threw her phone back in her purse and turned the shower on scalding hot.

Back to the grind.

As much as she hated getting up early, Alaina felt surprisingly eager. It was the feeling she had when she walked on stage; excitement, pleasure, and a pride in knowing she would bring joy to others. She wouldn't have believed it but she was actually looking forward to going to Heart House. It hadn't nearly been as bad as she expected, yes they were a bit loud and unruly but they were just teenagers. And when she'd begun to connect with them, it really had been amazing. Opera had given her so much and she couldn't imagine a life without it, she wanted these kids to have the opportunity to, to be amazed, to be impressed, to be inspired. . If she could inspire just one of them to attend a classical concert instead of a rock concert, then she'd done her job.

Feeling renewed, Alaina walked into the classroom. "Everyone sit down and shut off your phones. We're talking about settings today."

"It's too early to think." The Goth boy in the corner covered his head with his hood.

"I didn't get much sleep last night." A boy from the other corner whined.

Alaina wouldn't let them get to her. Not this time. "Sleep or no sleep, we're going around the world. Who wants to go first and tell me where your opera will be set?"

No one raised their hands. At least they weren't looking at their phones. "Well?" She scanned the room. Purple hair looked almost interested. What was her name again…"Jackie, what about you?"

Jackie shrugged. "I don't know. I was thinking like some castle in Europe."

"That's wonderful." Alaina wrote *castle in Europe* on the chalkboard. "Anyone else?"

"Mine's gonna be in the hood." The boy at the back shouted out. Everyone giggled.

Alaina paused, thinking. Should she discipline him? "What's your name?"

"John." He wouldn't make eye contact. His sweatshirt was ripped and stained across the front and he looked like he hadn't taken a shower in a few days. What kind of home did he come from? Had he eaten breakfast? She'd bet not. She couldn't imagine the kind of conditions some of these kids lived in.

"John, that's an excellent setting."

Then, she wrote *in the hood* next to Jackie's *castle*. "I'm sure you'll have a lot to write about." She gave him a steady stare as if to make sure he followed through.

"But, that's not a good place for an opera." A girl with a Yankees cap wearing sweatpants shouted from the third row.

"Says who?" Alaina gave the class her practiced mysterious grin. "Mozart set his opera *Abduction from the Seraglio* in a harem. You all know what that is, right? You can set your operas anywhere you like, the stranger…the better."

After she said that, more students raised their hand. She supposed they'd been afraid their ideas were 'dumb,' but after she'd accepted John's answer, they knew she wasn't going to make any of them feel bad. One after another, the settings kept coming.

A circus.

The beach.

A pirate ship.

Alaina had to write smaller and smaller to fit all of the answers on the board. The scope of their imaginations impressed her. These were talented kids. They might not have the same emotional and financial backing as her prep school friends, but that didn't stop their creativity.

She stood in front of the cluttered board and studied it with pride. She'd made this happen. An entire class of thirty high school kids were going to write an opera.

The bell rang, and she turned to the class and raised her eyebrows. "Your homework is the next step: heroes and villains."

CHAPTER SEVEN

Sabotage

Brett rubbed his eyes against the glare of the morning sun. He'd had to take a cold shower last night after his date with Alaina. Even then, he lay in bed unable to sleep, thinking about the way her soft lips hungered for more.

"Late night last night?" Phil knelt beside him as he measured the edge of the sidewalk.

Reality returned along with Phil's coffee breath. "You could say that."

Phil ran his hands through his salty gray hair. "Are you gonna tell me or not?"

Brett sighed. "Tell you what?"

"How your date went." Phil widened his eyes like it was obvious. It *was* obvious. Brett was procrastinating.

"It was fine." He continued his measurements. Can't have a crooked sidewalk, or the baby carriages would roll right off.

"*Fine* doesn't keep you up all night, does it?"

"Okay, it was more than fine." Brett gazed into the traffic, not seeing a single car. "It was perfect."

Phil smiled, probably wanting all the details. But Brett was not a kiss-and-tell kind of guy.

"So when are you two going out again?"

"I don't know." Brett stopped measuring. He couldn't concentrate with Phil bringing up the one problem he'd tried hard to avoid.

"You don't know?" Phil furrowed his bushy eyebrows.

Brett was tired of lying, and Phil had been his friend since he'd started on the job. He had to talk to someone. "There's one little problem. She thinks I'm three billion dollars richer."

Phil slapped his hand on his forehead. "It was the plane, wasn't it? I told you it'd be too much."

"No, it wasn't that. It's a long story."

Phil sat on the curb, pulled out a Hostess snack from his pocket, and opened a bag of donuts. "I'm on break. I've got time."

Brett put his equipment down. He was already ahead of schedule. A few minutes wouldn't hurt. He told his friend about Mrs. DeBarr, how he'd posed as her son, and what had happened at the auction.

Phil shook his head, white donut sugar going everywhere. "Man, you're in deep."

"Tell me about it."

"Why don't you just tell this Alaina the truth? I know you might get the old lady in trouble, but this seems more important than some business arrangement- which- if I understood your story correctly- she isn't paying you anything by the way."

"I didn't do it for money. I did it to help the fundraiser. Besides, I feel bad for Mrs. DeBarr. Her own son stood her up. I don't want to make her life any harder."

Phil crinkled the wrapper and stuffed it in his pocket. "No offense to the rich, but how hard can life be when you're a billionaire?"

Brett paused. He had a point.

"By the way, I called her." Phil leaned back against a fire hydrant and crossed his hands behind his head.

"Called who?" Brett's mind still swam with thoughts of Alaina. "Sarah."

Oh no, here he goes again. They'd be here all day and no one would have a sidewalk to walk on. Never mind the building they were supposed to be renovating behind them. "And?"

"She wasn't home. The phone rang and rang, and then I got her answering machine."

Brett crossed his arms across his chest. "So what did you say?" Phil glanced away. "Nothing. I hung up."

Across the street, a black limo parked in front of a taxi and the cab driver beeped, shouting profanities. Brett checked to see if he could read the license plate, but the angle made it too difficult to make anything out. He made himself focus. His friend needed him. "How's she supposed to know you called?"

"I froze up, man. I had no idea what to say. It's been so long." He covered his face with his hand. "I felt like an idiot."

Brett put a hand on his shoulder. Who was he to be telling Phil to speak up when he couldn't even tell Alaina the truth? "It's all right. Try again tonight. This time have what you want to say written down on a piece of paper."

Phil nodded. "You think I'm doing the right thing?"

"All I know is you talk about her all the time. You'll regret it if you never give it a second chance."

The door to the limo opened, and Mrs. DeBarr stepped out wearing a leather coat, a long gray skirt and pearls as big as quarters. She walked to the street corner, then crossed over to his side. Brett gave his friend his equipment. "Hold this for me. I've got something to finish."

Phil glanced at the older woman and nodded. "I got ya covered."

Brett met Mrs. DeBarr on the corner. When she saw him, she smiled like she was greeting an old friend. "How's my dear son this morning?" She reached up to give him a kiss on the cheek.

He leaned down for her kiss, feeling a little out of place. He didn't deserve it. He wasn't her son. "A little tired, but good."

She led him into a coffee shop, where a line of people waited at the counter. Almost all of the tables were full. Some people sat, reading their iPads, while others chatted and laughed. Brett didn't have time for this, but he had to ask her one thing.

He waited as she ordered a latte. Mrs. DeBarr gave the server a five and told him to keep the change. She turned back to Brett. "I take it your date went well?"

"It did." Brett reached in his pocket and handed her the credit card. "Alaina was very happy."

"Good." She glanced at him. "Do you want anything? Coffee, tea, a pastry?"

"No. Thank you."

She studied his face as she waited for her drink. "You seem preoccupied."

Brett stuck his hands in his jeans pockets. It was now or never. He'd probably never see Mrs. DeBarr again. "It's just that...I really like Alaina. I need to tell her the truth."

Mrs. DeBarr blinked as though surprised. "You have feelings for her?"

"I do. And it seems like she feels the same." Inviting him into her apartment was a big hint.

"I see." She reached over the counter and grabbed her latte. "That does complicate matters seeing as we've been invited to a luncheon this Saturday."

"We?" Brett narrowed his eyes.

"Everyone loved you. Mrs. Schuster found the bidding show to be so entertaining, she invited you to be the guest of honor at the Movers and Groovers awards luncheon to benefit cancer research. She wants you to speak about the importance of raising funds for those in need. She thinks your charisma will get people to listen."

"I agreed to one event and one event only." He lowered his voice so only she could hear. "I can't keep pretending to be your son."

Mrs. DeBarr pulled him to a quiet corner of the coffee shop. "This is for cancer research. You know how many people die of cancer each year?"

Brett shrugged. He didn't want to know. "Why don't you just give them the money?"

She smiled. "If only it was that easy. I can donate, and I do. But I'm only one person. Imagine ten other women like me all supporting the same cause, and then they each tell one of their friends. That makes twenty. And so on and so forth. But to get them interested in the first place, you have to get their attention. People want a social event, they want a show. You have to keep them talking, keep them involved in the cause. It's not a sprint, it's a marathon. A life-long marathon."

As much as her spiel made sense, Brett couldn't be part of it. "I'm not a spokesperson, I'm a construction worker."

She looked at him with such fondness, he almost felt like her son. "You could be so much more."

Brett shifted on his feet, suddenly uncomfortable. "What if I don't want to be?"

"That would be a shame." Mrs. DeBarr turned away. "I can't make you help me. As much as I want you to be, you're not my son."

A couple stood from their table in the corner.

"Goodbye, Brett." She moved quickly and sat down in their place. After rummaging through her purse, she took the plastic cover off her latte and sipped delicately. Despite her fancy clothes and stylish hair, she looked lost and alone.

The sadness in her last words held Brett in place. This lady was not his responsibility. Yet, he felt drawn to help her. His own mother would have wanted him to. Funnily enough, she would have said the same thing about him not living up to his potential. She used to urge him to leave Maine and start a life for himself in a big city like New York. But, he'd always reassure her he was happy logging like his father. The continuation of the family business gave him pride.

Until the fire took it all away.

Brett dragged himself over to the table and sat across from

Mrs. DeBarr. She looked up with one eyebrow raised, and he sighed in defeat.

"Exactly what do you want me to do?"

***

Alaina left the school and took a taxi straight to her first rehearsal at the Met. As the cab wove around parked cars and pedestrians, she took out her phone and checked for missed calls.

None.

No matter. He wouldn't call the next day away way. That would be too desperate. Besides, he was probably busy in his office buying and selling stocks. Hopefully, he'd thought of her sometime between the Dow Jones and the FTSE.

The cab pulled up in front of the Met and she paid and stepped out to the sound of raucous construction work. Alaina stared across the street with venom. The street looked worse now than it had done before they began work. The sidewalk was all torn up, and scaffolding covered the front of the office building. Or what was left of it. Not only that, but they took up several precious parking spaces with their loading trucks.

Honestly, couldn't they work at night when there wasn't as much traffic?

The same broad shouldered man she'd seen yesterday looked up suddenly and froze, measuring tools in hand. Was he staring at her?

She narrowed her eyes, but his hard hat cast his face in shadow. Before she could get a closer look, he disappeared under the scaffolding.

Strange. She didn't know anyone in construction. Yet, somehow he seemed familiar. If she wasn't dating Lance, than she'd walk over and say hi. Construction workers weren't all that bad. They'd almost completed the portion of the walkway in front of the opera house, and she had to admit it looked gorgeous. So all that noise and commotion had been worth the fuss.

Alaina checked her watch. No time to stay and find out who he was. She had the most important rehearsal of her life to attend. Normally the singers would rehearse with a pianist first, but she'd been chosen last minute, so she had to launch right into the final set of dress rehearsals complete with the costumes, the set and the orchestra.

As she entered the theater, descending through the rows and rows of red seats, a flute played an arpeggio, a few singers warmed up, and some violins tuned. Anxious nerves bubbled up inside her. Normally she didn't get nervous for a rehearsal, but this wasn't just any rehearsal.

A beautiful forest of fake trees inhabited by large papier mâché animals decorated the stage. A twilight backdrop with sparkling stars hung in the back. The man who played Papageno stood with his prop flute wearing a cape of feathers, practicing his moves while a girl dressed as a giant flamingo hopped around.

Bianca sat on the edge of the stage in a pink, sequined tank and skinny jeans talking with the conductor. Her gaze became chilly when she saw Alaina. Bianca ended her conversation, and the conductor walked away to speak with the concertmaster.

Alaina's heart sped, and her throat tightened. She made a beeline for the restrooms, needing just a few moments to regroup. She threw her bags, her purse and her coat on the sink and chose a stall to sit down and slow her breathing.

The door opened and pink high heels clicked on the floor. "Hello, Alaina. I saw you come in."

Damn. All she wanted was a few moments of peace. She hadn't had any time to warm up because she'd been volunteering all day. "Hi, Bianca."

"Excited for the first rehearsal?" The heels walked to the sink. She must have been putting more make-up on, because she didn't use the faucet.

"Of course." Alaina tried not to sound too overeager. She'd sung in rehearsals all the time, just not at the most famous opera house in the United States. Back in her Julliard days, she used to pass by the massive stone structure and daydream of singing on the grand stage, surrounded by tiers of balconies of applauding audience members.

"See you in there." Bianca left without so much as turning on the water. Had she come in here just to taunt her?

Alaina gathered her wits and opened her stall. She washed her hands and dug in her purse to freshen her makeup. After a few touches of foundation, she dug out her lipstick. She smeared it over her lips, feeling like the tip wasn't as sharp as the last time she'd used it. Had she jammed the cap on? It also smelled a little funny- more like chemicals and less like the usual vanilla scent. When she licked her lips, they tasted horrible.

Alaina pulled the lipstick away and read the expiration date. Nope. Still fine for the next six months. She'd only bought it a few weeks ago. Guess she wasn't shopping at that CVS again.

She tossed the lipstick in the garbage and returned to the theater, taking a seat in the front row. The orchestra tuned while the conductor reviewed his score on the podium.

He tapped his baton on his stand and announced, "Act One."

So they were working in order for the first dress rehearsal. She had some time to relax before she had to sing. Alaina leaned back in her seat and enjoyed the show.

The orchestra began with ominous tones as a giant serpent controlled by six people moved on the stage. The hero, Tamino, dodged the attack and began to sing. Even though the libretto was in German, Alaina understood.

"Help me, or I am lost!"

Damn, he sounded good. The tenor playing Tamino had a biography twice as long as hers with credits spanning the globe. His voice boomed through the highest balcony, pure and clear with luscious vibrato.

"There is no escape from this serpent." Tamino ran across the stage as violins raced down 16th note runs.

"Closer and closer it comes!"

The snake dipped its head and Tamino ducked. "Someone help me!"

The lighting moved to the back of the stage where three women wearing giant headdresses in purple, blue, and red raised their right hands. "Die monster, by our power!"

Alaina's lips tingled. She raised her finger and touched them. Numb. It didn't even feel like it was her mouth. What was happening? She hadn't been to the dentist lately.

Panic wrapped cool fingers around her throat. How could she pronounce the German words without any feeling in her lips? She slapped her mouth lightly, and then more firmly.

Nothing. Her lips were flabs of dead meat.

Alaina glanced at the stage. The three women still fought over which one of them stayed to watch over Tamino. She had time. Her entrance was thirty minutes into the opera- that's if Altez decided not to go back and fix anything.

Bianca's pink sequins caught her gaze from the edge of the stage. The blond bombshell smirked as though she was already in character as the Queen of the Night. Could she see Alaina's panic?

Embarrassment flamed in Alaina's cheeks. She bolted to the bathroom. Even though she felt as though she'd lost the bottom half of her face, she looked perfectly fine in the mirror. Dread crawled in her stomach like a worm, twisting. Should she call the emergency room?

The lipstick!

Alaina dug through the garbage. It must have something to do with the lipstick. Underneath some tissues, she found the lipstick alongside a tube of *Mr. Numb*. Alaina picked up the tube, reading the fine print on the back. "Super strong tattoo topical numbing cream anesthetic with a non-oily cream base. Numbs for up to three hours. Great for tattoos, tattoo removal, piercings, bikini waxing, etc.

Holy shit. Bianca had sabotaged her. While Alaina sat in the stall, Bianca must have smeared her lipstick in the cream. Back at Julliard, Alaina developed the habit of applying her makeup right before she performed. Bianca had always called her vain. That opera witch must have remembered and planned accordingly.

Dammit! What was going to do? Alaina tried to sing in the bathroom, and the words came out slurred, like she was some drunk from the street. Sure, she could go out there and point the finger at Bianca, but her nemesis would just deny it and everyone would think Alaina was some type of paranoid psycho. Or worse, they'd think she sabotaged herself just to get out of the first rehearsal.

Think, Alaina, think. She popped her head back into the theater. They were still rehearsing the scene with the three women. She had some time. But not three hours. In three hours everyone would be packing up.

She ran back to the restroom and washed all of the lipstick off her mouth. She hadn't applied too much, so maybe she'd regain feeling sooner than three hours. Alaina contorted her lips, making faces in the mirror to try to wake them up. She couldn't feel the tip of her tongue where she'd licked her lips, but she did have some feeling in the middle and back of her mouth.

She buzzed her lips together, then launched into the warm ups that didn't use the lips muscles. Slowly, she tried a "Mi, mo, my, ma, moo" exercise she'd learned from her teacher back in high school. It sounded more like, "E, o, I, a oo."

Alaina slammed her fist on the sink. What the hell was she going to do? What would be worse; not showing at all, or showing up and singing like an idiot?

She tiptoed back into the theater. Bianca stood on stage as the Queen of the Night, singing to Tamino. In her spidery, black gown, she looked more like a witch than any Halloween costume could ever pull off.

The conductor stopped the orchestra suddenly. "No, no, no! More *dolce*, more *rubato*. Yes, you're an evil, headstrong woman attempting murder and you'll stop at nothing- even using your own daughter until Sarastro is dead. But, here you're trying to plead to Tamino to save her. You have to sound convincing." The conductor covered his heart with his hand. "You miss her, you're worried about her. Tamino can't know your true intentions."

Alaina bit her lip. Like Bianca had any of those feelings for her. She'd be glad if Alaina fell off the stage and broke her neck. The irony was, her hatred toward Alaina shone right through her own singing and today, it was bringing her down.

Alaina took a seat, biding her time. They rehearsed the scene again and again until Bianca' voice grew hoarse. By the time they moved on to Tamino's meeting with Papageno, Alaina could feel the tip of her tongue against her front teeth.

"Here's your costume, my dear."

An older woman stood beside her holding a strapless, glimmering, white gown reminding Alaina of a cross between a wedding dress and a ballerina's Tutu. "Hi, I'm Catherine, the head designer. I've made it to the specifications you gave Altez. I hope it fits."

"It's 'eutiful." Alaina covered her mouth at the mispronunciation, but the older woman didn't seem to notice over Bianca's screaming voice.

Alaina slipped backstage to the dressing room. After she squeezed herself into the tight bodice, she massaged her lips and tried singing again. This time the words came out better, and she heaved a sigh of relief. She checked her figure in the mirror, pleased. The dress brought out all the right curves while smoothing over the ones she didn't want seen. The glimmering bodice blossomed into the layers and layers of light chiffon. She looked amazing.

Bianca had taken so long to get her part right, she'd thwarted her own plan.

Alaina left the bathroom and walked backstage, rehearsing her lines in her head as the three women presented Tamino with the magic flute that could bring peace on earth.

The stage director led Alaina into place beside the man playing the evil Monostatos and his lackeys. She took a deep breath as

Tamino and Papageno sang their last words, and then sprang into action, running across the stage away from Monostatos.

"Your life is over." Monostatos taunted her with a prop dagger.

"I'm not afraid of death." Alaina's voice rang clear, pronouncing the German words perfectly. Her confidence increased. "I am sad only for my mother. She will surely die of grief."

Yeah, right. More like die of disappointment.

As Alaina sang, she watched Bianca. The Queen of the Night crossed her arms and narrowed her eyes. Sure, Alaina had won this round. But, Bianca wouldn't give up this easily. From now on Alaina had to watch her back.

CHAPTER EIGHT

Improvisation

Brett adjusted the collar of his new, navy Armani suit- a present from Mrs. DeBarr. Even though he looked like a million bucks, he felt cheap and sleazy. How long could he keep this pretense up?

A black limo pulled up to the curb in front of his apartment. Some of the neighborhood kids playing with sidewalk chalk glanced up and stared. The limo looked like a rare, sleek beast next to the scuffed up Toyotas and Chevrolets parked on the side of the street.

He opened the door and slid into the leather seat. The interior smelled like pine, reminding him of home.

Mrs. DeBarr smiled warmly. She wore an elegant, white business suit with a red and blue striped scarf. "How's my dear boy today?"

"Nervous." He adjusted the cuffs of his suit. "I've never given a speech. I have no idea what to say."

"Leave that to me." She reached in her purse and pulled out a wad of index cards.

He took the cards, read the first couple, then slid them into his inside breast pocket. "Thanks."

"Thank you. Your presence at this event will surely draw some big donations."

Anxiety along with hope crawled up his spine. "Will Alaina be there?"

Mrs. DeBarr shrugged. "I had no idea she was coming to the first fundraiser. To tell you the truth, from what I'd heard about her, I didn't think she cared."

"She does now." Defensiveness reared up inside him. "She's a kind hearted woman once you get to know her."

"You really do like her, don't you?" Mrs. DeBarr smiled. Her certainty unnerved him.

Brett glanced away. He hadn't called Alaina since their date. He didn't know what to say if he couldn't tell her the truth. Every word out of his mouth cemented him further in the lie.

They drove downtown to the Metropolitan Banquet Facility. Brett had walked by the massive building on one of his initial tours of New York, but he never thought he'd be going inside. Not that he wanted to. He'd much rather be hiking or canoeing. But, he'd left that life behind.

The limo dropped them off by the revolving glass doors. Brett helped Mrs. DeBarr from the limo and up the steps. "So you usually attend these events on your own?"

Mrs. DeBarr nodded and tapped her hand on his arm. "It's nice to have company."

He wondered where Mr. DeBarr was, then thought it best not to ask. Whenever someone asked him about his parents an uncomfortable weight fell on the conversation.

They passed a lobby with chandeliers and marble floors and took the elevator to the south hall on the twenty-seventh floor, a massive room at the corner of the building surrounded by glass. The city stretched out all around them as they entered, the skyscrapers reflecting the early afternoon sun. White tablecloths decorated with pink and red flower arrangements spread before them.

Brett scanned the room for Alaina. Most of the people

congregated by the windows. They sipped wine and chatted in social circles. Two older ladies came and took Mrs. DeBarr away, leaving him to stand on his own with a crowd of people who thought he was someone else.

A high-pitched voice came from his left. "My, my. Look who just walked in. The talk of the auction."

Brett turned around reluctantly. Ms. Barbie strutted toward him in a pink and black polka dot cocktail dress way too short for her long legs. Brett made sure not to look down and tried to remember her name.

"Bianca, remember?" She offered her hand. A waft of sweet perfume that reminded him of bubblegum permeated the space around him, giving him the urge to choke. "I hope you didn't have too much fun on your date."

He glanced around nervously for Alaina, hoping she hadn't spotted him with Bianca. "Just enough to make it worth the price paid."

"Oh, you're such a tease." She hit his chest with her hand. "If only I could have stayed in the bidding."

Thank God she didn't. He turned away, scouring his brain for any kind of way out.

"By the way, a friend of mine works in your office. She says you just got back from a trip to China?"

China? Brett coughed. "I apologize. There's a tickle in my throat. If you'll excuse me."

Before she could respond, he slipped toward the bathroom at the back of the room. That's when he saw Alaina sitting by herself at the back table, staring across the city with a melancholy pout that broke his heart. It was as if she was searching for something or someone in the chaos. Maybe him.

His heart skipped a beat. He hoped it *was* him.

She wore a simple sleeveless blue dress that fanned out around her calves, contrasting with her sunset hair. A dab of blush brought out her high cheekbones. She looked absolutely, flawlessly gorgeous.

Brett paused, wondering if he should approach her or run in the other direction, but the pull was too strong and he couldn't resist. He stepped toward her. "Alaina?"

She whirled around and blinked in surprise. "Lance?"

He gestured to the seat beside her, wishing she knew his true name. "Is this seat taken?"

"No." She pulled out the chair. "I came alone."

He sat in the seat beside her, wanting to take her hand. Instead, he threaded his fingers together on the tabletop. "I'm sorry I haven't called."

She glanced down as sadness tinged her eyes. "You must have been busy."

Guilt poured over him. He'd hurt her feelings. *Busy trying to figure out what to do.* "I wanted to call."

"You did?" The corner of her mouth curved.

"More than anything."

She reached across the table and took his hand. It was as if no time had passed since their kiss. The heat still sizzled between them in full force.

Hope crossed her face. "I don't suppose they'll be auctioning another date?"

"Sadly, not." He leaned toward her and dropped his voice. "Today they have me giving a speech."

She studied his face and teased him with a smirk. "You sound like you don't want to."

"I feel like I'm in fifth grade again, about to give a report."

Alaina laughed. "I'm surprised. I thought you would have been a stellar student."

Maybe the real Lance was, but Brett had always been more interested in the outdoors. "Let's just say I wasn't the teacher's pet."

"I like that." Alaina rubbed her thumb across his forefinger. "A trouble maker."

Desire stirred deep in his gut. "I wouldn't go that far."

She set her elbow on the table and placed her chin on her free hand. "How far would you go?"

Applause erupted behind them. Mrs. DeBarr had taken the podium, and smiled as her colleagues and friends took their seats at the tables around her. Lance breathed in relief with a mixture of disappointment. He liked where their conversation was headed. Alaina had a way of turning small talk into fire.

Mrs. DeBarr introduced him, and everyone turned in their seats. Alaina squeezed his arm. "Break a leg with your report."

"Thanks." Her little joke gave him the courage to stand. Brett left the table and walked to the podium. His chest tightened, and his suit felt a little too tight. He'd meant to go over the rest of the index cards, but Alaina had distracted him. He'd just have to wing it.

"Hello, everyone." His voice boomed over the microphone, and he pulled it back. "Thanks for inviting me here today. I'll make this short so you can get to your lunch. I know we're all hungry."

Great. That sounded like the dumbest thing he'd ever said. But, the audience laughed lightly. This was an easier crowd than his fellow schoolmates. Brett slipped the cards from his pocket and placed them on the podium. "Today I'll be talking about the importance of fundraising."

Boy, this did feel like some school presentation. Back in sixth grade he had done a report on President Woodrow Wilson, and had decided to dress up like him all the way down to the business suit and thin-rimmed glasses. Today he felt no less ridiculous.

Brett put the index cards down. He didn't need them back then, and he didn't need them now. "This isn't about statistics and reports. It's about people. People in need. People who have a hole in their heart so big, they could drown right in it."

He paused, scanning the audience. Bianca sipped her wine, only half paying attention. In the back Alaina smiled encouragingly. Surprise widened Mrs. DeBarr's eyes, but she nodded for him to continue.

Brett took a deep breath. His fingers shook, but he knew what

69

he had to say. "I'm no stranger to tragedy. When it struck, it blind-sided me so hard I lost who I was and any meaning in my life." He glanced at Alaina. "Only through the kindness of others could I learn to live again. And that's what this is about. Not giving money to a cause for a tax deduction or to get your photo in the papers, but reaching out to real people, telling them they're not alone."

He stepped back as if he'd just run a marathon, and waited for the result. "Thank you for listening."

Mrs. DeBarr stood and started clapping, then her whole table followed her example. Alaina stood in the back, and then the table beside her, and the one beside that one until everyone in the room stood and clapped.

Brett's face grew hot as surprise spread through him. He'd spoken from the heart, but he hadn't expected it to touch so many people. Mrs. DeBarr came up and opened her arms. He leaned down and hugged her, and she whispered in his ear, "I knew you could do it. Well done!"

She took the microphone, and he walked back to the table with Alaina and sat down.

Alaina leaned over. "I'm so sorry. I had no idea you'd been through so much."

What had he done? He couldn't even speak to his best friend about what had happened and now he'd just shared his deepest, darkest moment with a bunch of strangers. He didn't want their pity.

Brett sat back in his seat as the waiters and waitresses brought in plates of herb-crusted chicken. "I hadn't meant to. I should have just read the index cards."

"No." Alaina hadn't picked up her fork. She stared at him in awe. "What you did up there was perfect."

After lunch, Mrs. DeBarr took the podium one last time thanking everyone for coming. She held up a clear fishbowl full of small pieces of paper. "And now we get to see who's won the tickets."

70

"What tickets?" Brett folded his napkin on the table.

"Two tickets for a weekend getaway at the White Mountain Lodge in northern New Hampshire."

Brett perked up. The famous White Mountain Lodge? He'd always wanted to go there, and it was peak foliage season. Located at the base of Mount Washington, the highest peak in the Northeastern United States, the area had numerous hiking trails and amazing waterfalls. "Too bad I didn't enter." Like he could even afford the raffle ticket.

"You did enter." Alaina pointed to his lap. "Under your seat there's a number. Those are the numbers she's picking through right now."

"Really?" Hope rose inside his chest.

Alaina laughed. "Your face reminds me of Charlie when he's about to open the candy bar to see if he has a golden ticket."

Brett tried to contain his excitement. "I've been wanting to go there for some time." He rubbed his hands up and down his legs. His palms had grown sweaty.

Mrs. DeBarr stirred the small papers with her hand. She picked one from the bottom and drew it out of the fish bowl slowly. "Seat number thirty-four."

Everyone ducked under their seats to have a look. Brett followed their example, feeling a little foolish to want something so badly that he had no idea existed just a moment ago. His seat read fifty-one. His lungs deflated.

Alaina watched him rise. "No luck?"

He shook his head. "Fifty-one."

"That must mean I'm fifty-two then." Alaina sipped her wine. "No need to check."

Mrs. DeBarr took the microphone. "Still no winner. Keep looking, people!"

Brett stared at Alaina and she shook her head. "Naw. It can't be me. I sat all the way in the back."

He couldn't believe she hadn't moved yet. "Check your seat."

"Oh, all right." She put her glass down and fell to her knees. She stuck her head under her seat, then jumped up. "Bingo!"

"Congratulations!" Mrs. DeBarr waved the piece of paper in the air. "Make sure you see me before you leave to get your prize."

Alaina collapsed back in her seat. "I can't believe I won. I've never won anything in my life." She looked at him and her eyes brightened. "The tickets are for two. Looks like you'll be going after all."

Brett blinked in surprise. She'd skipped the whole invitation part and assumed he was going. He sure as hell wanted to go, but bells of reason rang in his ears. He didn't want to spend all that time pretending he was someone else.

Alaina stiffened. "What? You don't have time?"

"No. It's not that." Brett ran his hands through his hair, trying to figure out what to do. Alaina's alarm broke his heart. How could he let her down? Besides, did he want her going with anyone else besides him? An ugly streak of jealousy surged inside him. Nope. Not in a million years. This was his chance to get to know her. He pushed aside all his fears. "I'd love to go with you."

"Great!" She hit her hand on the table like a judge declaring a final decision. "The tickets are for next weekend."

"Next weekend?" That didn't give him much time to straighten things out.

"That's right. I'll have to buy a pair of hiking shoes." She winked. "No more high heels for our dates."

Alaina in hiking shoes? He couldn't wait.

At the end of the luncheon he pulled Mrs. DeBarr aside. They walked to the corridor outside the room where no one else would overhear. She patted his arm, beaming with a bright smile. "You were marvelous."

Brett shifted uncomfortably. He didn't want to be marvelous, he just wanted to do the job and get out of this situation. "I'm sorry I didn't follow your cards."

"Nonsense." She leaned on the windowsill. "Everyone thought you were speaking of my husband."

"Mr. DeBarr?"

She nodded solemnly and her eyes grew watery. She dug in her purse, brought out a wadded tissue and dabbed at the corners of her eyes. She looked as though she were holding herself together with threads.

Brett loosened his collar as the walls pressed in around him. Did he want to ask? No. Bringing up another tragedy only made him think of his own. Besides, it wasn't his place. He was already too involved with this old woman. Tears or not, he had to pull out the stops and lay down the law. She'd helped him meet Alaina, but if he intended on keeping her, he had to stop Mrs. DeBarr's little game.

"Listen, you know Alaina won the tickets to the resort?"

Mrs. DeBarr nodded, her diamond earrings swinging. "Yes, I do."

"She's asked me to go with her."

"That's wonderful." Mrs. DeBarr opened her purse. "You'll need my credit card."

"No." Brett took her hand. "I can't go out with her any longer under this pretense. I have to tell her the truth."

Mrs. DeBarr wiped her forehead and stuffed the tissue back in her purse. Her hands shook. "I'm afraid you can't do that."

"Why the hell not?" Brett glanced behind his shoulder. He'd raised his voice a little too loud. Bianca was at the opposite end, pressing the button for the elevator. Had she overheard?

"Yes, yes, I'll be right there." She brought her cell phone down from her ear and stuffed it in her purse.

Brett breathed a sigh of relief. Thank god she'd been on the phone.

Mrs. DeBarr didn't skip a beat. "I need you more than anything now. Mrs. Shields has asked if you could speak at the next luncheon."

Brett dropped his voice. "The *next* luncheon? There isn't going to bed another luncheon because I'm not your son. I agreed to one night, remember?"

Mrs. DeBarr glanced at the door to the banquet hall. Her voice took on a conspirator's tone. "How well do you know Alaina?"

He shrugged. He'd just met her last Monday night at the cocktail party.

"What do think she'll do if you tell her the truth?"

Brett glanced at his shiny, expensive shoes- shoes Mrs. DeBarr had bought for him, shoes he couldn't afford with three months' pay. Would Alaina still be interested in him if she knew he wore construction boots instead of Oxford's?

Mrs. DeBarr nodded. "She'd probably be really upset and demand her money back. Then all of these ladies would do the same, withdrawing everything they'd donated today. I can see the front page of the New York Times: local philanthropist and construction worker deceive the masses. I wouldn't be able to fundraise for anything again."

Brett clenched his hands into fists. She should have thought of that before she dressed him in her son's clothes. *He* should have thought of the consequences before he'd taken her offer. But now here they were, stuck in the lie. "We should come clean now before it gets any worse."

"No." She grabbed his arm, her eyes wide with desperation. "Not yet."

Brett narrowed his eyes. She wasn't telling him something. "What's the rush? Why is this so important to you right now?"

She sighed and her shoulders fell forward. "It's time you meet Mr. DeBarr."

CHAPTER NINE

Time

The door to the banquet room opened, and a bunch of people flooded the hall, thanking Mrs. DeBarr for bringing such a wonderful guest speaker. Between hugs and handshakes, Mrs. DeBarr turned back to Brett. "Why don't we go back in and collect my things?"

"Good idea." He took her arm and cut a path through the crowd, leading her back to the hall. Once they were inside, he found her coat as she talked with the remaining guests.

He had so many questions, but he couldn't risk talking about their unique situation any further. The best thing to do was get to the limo, then work out this whole mess. The bottom line was that he cared about her, no matter what she'd put him through, and he had to know what fueled her desperation.

"There you are. I thought you were going to leave without saying goodbye." Alaina popped up beside them.

"Of course not." Brett cursed silently. In all of the drama, he'd forgotten about Alaina.

"Are you doing anything tonight?"

Mrs. DeBarr gave him a scolding look as she talked with two

other guests. "My...mother and I have other plans."

"Oh, I see." Alaina fidgeted with an emerald ring on her second finger, probably thinking of some way to prolong their conversation. Damn, she looked cute. "I had a nice time today."

"Me, too." Brett wished he could stay.

She brought out her phone. "By the way, I need a number to call you about our plans."

A number? Great. All he had was his apartment number, which could be traced right down to the dingy brick building on the other side of town. "Why don't I call you?"

Alaina frowned. "Sure. You still have my card, right?" She raised one eyebrow skeptically.

"Right on my desk." That was not a lie. He'd looked at the card every morning when he got up and every night before he fell asleep.

"We must be going." Mrs. DeBarr gave Alaina a curt smile.

"I'm sorry, ma'am." Alaina stepped back. She turned to Brett. "I'll see you later."

"You can count on it." He watched Alaina leave, hoping his lie with Mrs. DeBarr wouldn't get him and Alaina.

"She's a little too pushy for my tastes." Mrs. DeBarr adjusted her scarf over her coat.

"You could have been nicer." She reminded him of his own mom- no girl was ever good enough.

"Pushy means nosey, which could mean trouble." Mrs. DeBarr gestured toward the door. "Our limo awaits."

They drove to the Lower Manhattan Hospital in silence. Mrs. DeBarr seemed preoccupied, playing with the pearls around her neck and staring out the window. Brett wasn't about to ask questions. He'd get his answers soon enough.

At the hospital they took the elevator to a room in the corner. An older man with wispy white hair, black eyebrows and a prominent, boney nose lay with a curtain of plastic all around him. A breathing tube had been hooked up to his mouth, and several tubes sprouted from his arms. He wore a hospital gown. A white sheet covered his legs.

Compassion overwhelmed Brett. The man looked so fragile, so small. Brett never had a chance to see his parents' age. It would have been hard to see them like this. He couldn't decide which was worse – to have them disappear overnight, or waste away one breath at a time. "I'm sorry."

Mrs. DeBarr touched the side of the plastic gently. "They've slowed his heart rate, his breathing, and all his bodily systems to slow the progression of the cancer."

She trailed her fingers along the glass. "It's a new research program they're trying. We could have had a few months with him awake, or a year or two with him asleep while they try to find a cure."

"How long's it been?"

"Six months. I've invested all I could in research of all kinds. But, it's going to take a lot more money, effort, and awareness than I have to find a cure."

All at once, he understood her desperation in making him impersonate her son and bringing him to the luncheon. If that was his dad, his mom, or his love in there, he'd fundraise every penny he could.

"How does the real Lance feel about this?"

"You have to know Lance- he's practical and gets right down to business. Sure, he's upset. But, he believes it's his dad's time to go. He thinks I'm crazy for stretching out the inevitable, for trying too hard."

Brett took her hands. "You're not crazy. You're in love."

Unshed tears glistened in her eyes. "So you won't tell Alaina?"

Did he have a choice? He couldn't turn this old woman in. He just had to make sure Alaina would understand. He had to give their relationship more time, then he could tell her the truth. "I'll hold off, for a little while."

She sighed with relief. "And the next luncheon?"

He glanced away. There was only so many of these things he

could go to before people started asking questions or someone who knew the real Lance would cry wolf. "One more."

"Thank you. You don't know how much this means to me."

He had an idea. He'd lost people, too. But, he wasn't about to talk about it now. "No problem. Anything I can do to help."

The fancy façade she usually wore broke down, revealing a vulnerable side he'd only glimpsed at before. "You've already helped me so much, not only appearing at these functions, but by spending time with me." She reached out and touched his arm. "It's like I have my son back."

Compassion poured through him, and for the first time, he felt like a son again. How could he deny her anything now? Brett placed a hand on hers. "Whatever you need, I'll be there."

She kissed the plastic and they exited the room.

Brett looked in the other rooms they passed seeing family members at the foot of each bed. Would it have been easier for him if he'd gotten a chance to say goodbye to his parents?

"I can understand the need for research."

She nodded. "Only when it happens to someone you care about you begin to understand."

Helping people raise money for cancer research was all good, but lying to do it still didn't sit right with him. "What would Lance say if he found out I was running around impersonating him?"

She waved her hand. "To tell you the truth, he's so involved in his business, I don't think he'd care. I told him you took his place at the auction, and he didn't bat an eye. He'd probably thank you for keeping me busy. You know how many of these things I've bugged him about coming to?"

Brett shook his head. If he ever met the real Lance, he'd have a thing or two to say.

***

Alaina woke up Monday morning and checked her phone. No

call. All weekend. What kind of a guy goes so hot and cold all the time? It drove her crazy. So crazy she almost thought about marching into his office and knocking on his door.

It had something to do with his mother. The way they talked so hushed all the time was strange, like they were spies against the world. Was she controlling him?

If so, did Alaina want a mama's boy?

She thought back to their date at the lodge in Maine. Never had a man gone to such lengths to impress her. All the musicians she'd dated had simply invited her to their concert. It was so hard to get away from the classical music world and do something different. She could do that with Lance. He showed her the world outside of concert life in the quiet isolation of the deep forest. Sure, she'd have to get used to the rocks and the bugs, but she always liked a challenge. Lance was modest and a laid back; completely different to all the other guys she'd ever dated. He was a breath of fresh air in more ways than one. And their chemistry was amazing. Like rocket science on steroids.

So what if he was a mama's boy? If she could take Bianca's flak, then she could take a controlling mother-in-law.

It wasn't like his mother could follow them everywhere. All Alaina needed to do was get him alone again- and they'd have that time this coming weekend. She had to keep busy until then. He'd call. He said he would.

Alaina took a cab to Heart House. She opened her classroom door to loud chatter. She was about to shout for everyone to be quiet when she heard some of the conversations.

"My hero is going to be a rock star." John sat next to the girl with the Yankee's cap. Did she ever take it off?

"Yeah, well, my villain is going to be a pirate who chops off people's heads." She chewed a wad of bubblegum as she poked a whole in her desk.

"That's silly. You're copying the opera Ms. Amaldi talked about." John fired back.

Alaina positioned herself in front of their desks. "It's not silly at all."

The room quieted.

"This assignment is purely creative. Nothing will be called silly." She pointed her finger at the girl. "Not rock stars, or even pirates who chop off heads."

Jackie actually raised her hand from the back of the room. One of her long sleeves fell down, and ugly red scratch marks covered her wrist. Alaina's chest tightened. Had she done that to herself? "Yes, Jackie?"

Jackie lowered her arm and her sleeve covered the scars. "What are we doing today?"

Alaina blinked, trying to focus. She couldn't call this girl's problems out in front of the whole class. "Today we're talking about plot. A lot of times, the plot in an opera is so convoluted and complex, it takes several sittings to make sense. Maybe the composers did it on purpose- to get people to come back again and again."

A few kids laughed. Good. At least some of them were paying attention.

She continued, pacing the room. "Anyway, that's the fun of it. For instance, in the opera I'm singing in now, my character is Pamina. Pamina is abducted by the evil Sarastro and his slave, Monostatos. The opera opens with the prince, Tamino, being pursued by a monstrous serpent. Three ladies in the service of the Queen of the night, A.K.A. my character's mother, save him. When they leave to tell the queen, a bird catcher named Papageno appears and boasts that he killed the creature. The ladies come back, show Tamino a picture of Pamina and he falls in love at first sight. The Queen of the Night asks him to save Pamina, but she's really using her daughter to get at Sarastro. She hands Tamino a magic flute and Papageno some magic bells. While Tamino's looking for Pamina, Papageno saves her and learns from a high priest that the Queen of the night is actually the evil one. And that's only the beginning."

Most of their eyes glazed over. John shook his head, and Jackie crinkled her eyebrows. This time she didn't raise her hand. "That makes no sense."

Alaina spread both hands like she'd performed a magic trick. "That's the fun of it. Now, get your pencils out. During this class, I want you to come up with your own ludicrous stories- the crazier the better. I'll come around and help you out individually."

Alaina gave them a few minutes, and then started her rounds. When she got to Jackie, she tried not to glance at her wrists. "So what do you have?"

Jackie tapped her pencil on her desk. "I don't know. Something about a baroness in a British castle." She handed Alaina a piece of ripped notebook paper.

Lady Elizabeth Delacorte learns, after the untimely death of her husband, that he squandered all of their money on gambling. In order to keep her castle, she must win the hand of the older, brooding Lord of Yorkshire, but she secretly loves, Philip Sweeny, her chimney sweep.

Alaina nodded, impressed and gave her back the paper. "This is very good."

"Thanks." Jackie tore off a piece of the ratty paper. "I thought it up this morning after a dream I had."

"You have creative dreams."

Jackie shrugged like it didn't matter. But it did. Everyone's dreams mattered.

"I have time after school today if you'd like to sing for me. I'd love to hear you." Before, she would have done everything to her power to get out of that school as soon as possible and get back to her own life. Now, it was more important to her to keep these kids dreaming big and believing they could achieve something.

Jackie shrugged again. She lost some of her earlier hootspa. Was she worried Alaina would put her down? "I don't know. My mom wants me to get her cigarettes at the corner store."

"You're not old enough to buy cigarettes."

"The guy who owns the store knows me."

Alaina shook her head. What kind of seven-eleven manager sells cigarettes to a kid? What kind of mother sends her daughter out to get them for her? What was this world coming to? Her parents supported every whim she'd had, whether it was singing, tap dancing, or acting in commercials. Without them, she wouldn't be here today, singing at the Met and teaching music.

This kid needed a mom who supported her talents, not used her as a cigarette mobile.

Alaina put both hands on her hips. "You told me you would, so you can't back out. I'm not taking no for an answer. It will only take five minutes."

"Okay." Jackie nodded but looked away.

Alaina pointed a finger at her as she moved to the next desk. "If you don't show up, I'll have you sing in front of class."

But Jackie did show up, right on time when the bell hit two fifty five.

Alaina pushed the books to the side of her desk. She'd already prepared herself for the worst. No matter what came out of that girl's mouth, she'd say something positive. "Let's hear it."

Jackie dropped her backpack on the floor and started to sing some pop song Alaina had never heard of. But she wasn't listening to the words.

The girl had a bold and beautiful voice with a sweet vibrato that reminded Alaina of herself at that age. Her vocal range was impressive, and her center of pitch remained through the whole song. Her tone had true heart and soul, making Alaina wish she knew what the song was about.

After Jackie finished, Alaina stood and clapped. "You are marvelous."

"Really?"

Alaina nodded. "And I'm not just saying that either."

"A lot of good it does, being able to sing." Jackie picked up her backpack and turned to leave. A hopeless feeling washed over Alaina. Did her praise even matter?

"Where are you going?"

"To get my mom's cigarettes, remember?"

Alaina stood, pushing her chair back behind her. "Wait a second. Don't you want to take lessons, learn some real classical stuff, you know prepare for college auditions?"

"Pft." Jackie waved her off. "We don't have money for lessons, never mind college."

"But your mom has money for cigarettes."

"Cigarettes are cheap." She'd almost made it to the door.

Not if you bought them every day. That added up over time. Anger built inside her. She called after the girl. "You tell your mom you'll be coming home a half hour later sometimes."

Jackie turned around with attitude. "Why? Do I have some type of detention?"

Alaina crossed her arms, determination hardening inside her. If this cigarette mom wasn't going to take an interest in her daughter's talents, than she would. "No. Vocal lessons. I'm going to teach you myself. For free."

CHAPTER TEN

From Riches to Rags

Brett's muscles burned as he hauled a large plank to the workmen. It felt good to be working outside with his own two hands instead of schmoozing with New York's elite. This work was black and white. You followed the instructions, and rebuilt the building from the ground up. No shady, in-between half-truths or slippery slopes of moral dilemmas. It all made his head hurt.

"Have a good weekend?" Phil punched him in the shoulder.

"You could say that." He didn't want to go into all the nitty gritty details with Phil. His friend wasn't the most sensitive guy. He'd probably tell him to ditch the old lady and go for the girl. "You?"

"Naw." Phil drunk from a coffee mug that could have been a gas tank. He took one long sip, then wiped his chin. He looked five years older than when Brett had last seen him. His salty white-brown hair was tussled and greasy, and dark circles hung under his eyes.

Brett set down the plank and rubbed his hands on his jeans to get the sawdust off. "Why not?"

"Kept thinking about Sarah. I couldn't sleep. That, and I think I ate too much Chinese."

"Spare me the details." He took a seat next to Phil. "Why didn't you give her a call?"

"I did. Twice last week after work. She didn't answer."

A coworker stopped drilling in the background, and Brett lowered his voice. "Did you leave a message like I told you to?"

Phil glanced away into the traffic. "I had nothing to say."

Frustration surged up inside him. Phil was a great builder, but when it came to communication, he lacked willpower. "Course you have something to say. Tell her how much you've been thinking about her, or how you want to visit that museum with her."

Phil shrugged. "There's no point. What we had ended a long time ago. She's probably found someone else by now."

"What's the message on the machine say? Any other names?"

"No."

"There's your answer." Brett stood, picked up a bag of equipment and slung it over his shoulder. If Phil wasn't going to do anything about it, then this conversation had finished. Then, an idea brightened in his mind. "Give me your phone."

"Why? Need another swanky getaway?"

"No. Just give it to me."

Phil reached in his back pocket and handed Brett the phone.

Brett scrolled through the call log. Bingo. He hit the talk button and handed Phil the phone.

"What are you doing?" Phil's eyes widened when he saw who he was calling. "Not right now."

"Why not? You're on a break. If she's not home at night, maybe she's home during the day."

Phil blinked in surprise as he clutched the phone to his ear. "Hello, Sarah? It's Phil." He scurried behind the building where the drilling wasn't as loud.

Brett crossed his arms feeling smug. Phil might want to kill him later, but he'd probably thank him in the long run. If only his own problem was as easy to deal with.

He walked back to the sidewalk, where a team was flattening

the new pavement. Pedestrians walked around the work crew in an area he'd sectioned off from the street. In the crowd, a blonde head emerged with a bright pink headband.

Bianca?

Brett ducked under the scaffolding. Jesus. Had she seen him?

He had to move or she'd pass right by him. Brett pulled his hat down over his forehead. Where could he go? He have to risk passing her to go into the coffee shop. The other direction was a women's clothing store. No way was he going in there.

He glanced at the cement truck. The passenger seat lay open. Brett sprinted across the path, opened the door and slipped into the truck. Using the side mirror, he watched as Bianca passed.

Two days ago, Bianca had been standing behind him when he was talking to Mrs. DeBarr about *not being her son*, then she walks right by his construction site.

Brett rubbed his hand over his face. He had to be more careful before he let the hammer out of the bag.

"You look like you've seen a ghost." The driver stared at Brett. "You okay, son?"

"I'm fine." Brett shook his head. He'd take a ghost over Bianca any day.

***

Alaina's cab stopped in dead traffic. She checked her watch as anxiety crawled up her spine. Rehearsals began in fifteen minutes and she still had to change into her costume. It had been absolutely worth it to stay late and hear Jackie sing, but now her own career hung in the balance.

She tapped on the glass. "Can't you do something about it?"

"I can't do nothing, lady." The driver chewed the end of his cigar and honked at the car in front of him. He reminded her of Danny DeVito in the movie *Twins*. That crook would have done anything for money, even if he had to convince an innocent and naïve Arnold Schwarzenegger he was his long lost brother. *Wait a second…*

She slipped a hundred dollar bill under the glass. "What will this do?"

His eyes bugged out at the sight of the green. He backed up and took a sharp turn into the left turning lane, then when the light turned green, he gunned it right into the other lane, cutting off six cars.

Alaina gripped the door handle so hard her fingers turned white. *The things you do for your career.*

The cab peeled rubber and careened down some alley she didn't even know existed, then ran a red light. They reached the opera house with two minutes to spare. Thankful to still be alive, Alaina paid the driver with the hundred dollar bill and ran up the stairs. She broke through the doors as the concertmaster stood to tune the violins.

Thank goodness Pamina isn't in the beginning.

With any luck, the conductor would work in chronological order again.

She grabbed her gown from the costume rack and slipped into the bathroom. Never in her life had she taken off all her clothes so quickly. She threw the gown over her head and pulled the fabric down around her.

The waist got stuck over her breasts.

What the?

She'd just worn it last Friday. How could she have gained so many pounds?

"Altez wants Pamina in five minutes." One of the serpent holders announced from the bathroom door.

Nope. Not rehearsing in order today. "I'll be right there." Alaina gritted her teeth and squished her breasts flat. The fabric pulled against her chest, making her feel claustrophobic. How could she sing if she couldn't even take in a good breath?

She yanked, and the fabric ripped down the back as she pulled it over her breasts.

Shit.

How many rolls had she had eaten at the luncheon? Two, three? Still, not enough to cause a fabric explosion. All of her other clothes fitted, even her skinny jeans.

Unless…someone had altered her costume.

What was the head costume designer's name? *Catherine! That's it.*

Alaina stuck her head from the bathroom door and waved down the closest person while her naked backside grew cold. One of the musicians from the orchestra came over. "Get me Catherine, the head costume designer. I'm having a wardrobe malfunction!"

The musician looked at her like she was some crazy diva.

"Don't just stand there. Go now!" She used her most commanding tone.

He nodded and jogged off.

Alaina waited on the other side of the bathroom door while the seconds ticked away. Being late to rehearsal, not having time to warm up, and tearing your beautiful costume went against everything her vocal teacher had taught her to battle performance anxiety. She used to think her teacher was a little too overzealous. But she was right. She'd been thrown off by so much, she could hardly remember her name, never mind the German lyrics of the opera.

The door opened and Catherine came in. "What is it my dear?"

Alaina blinked back tears. "The costume doesn't fit anymore."

Catherine crinkled her gray eyebrows, reminding Alaina of a confused librarian. "But I made it to your exact specifications."

Alain turned around, exposing her bare butt. "What do you call this?"

"Oh my." Catherine's eyes widened as she pulled at either side of the fabric. "My work has been altered."

"Altered?"

She shook her head. "I don't understand. Only the cast is

allowed access to the costume room. But, these are not my stitches. Someone's taken the dress in."

Anger rode over Alaina in an ugly tidal wave. Bianca. She must have taken the dress home over the weekend and made her own alterations. That conniving little bitch.

"I'll fix it after rehearsal." Catherine pulled at the seams with no luck.

"After?"

"They're waiting for you on stage, my dear."

"Am I going to moon the orchestra?"

Catherine disappeared and reappeared with a red cape. The older woman draped it over Alaina's ripped bodice. "Here. You can say I made the suggestion."

"You've got to be kidding me."

She shook her head and gave her an encouraging smile. "Today Pamina is going to save the world."

Embarrassed and frazzled, Alaina struggled to hold her head up high as she walked on stage.

"An interesting choice of accessory. However, you've given your character too much credit. Pamina is hardly superwoman." Bianca smirked from backstage. A few of the pink flamingos laughed.

Alaina ignored her.

Altez raised an eyebrow as she took her place, but didn't comment on her wardrobe change. Alaina assumed her pose and signaled she was ready to begin. Tamino turned his back on her, and the strings began with a sad pulse of sound.

Focus. Remember those words. She'd been singing this aria for years, ever since her first recital in high school. She calmed herself, and the words came like an old folk rhyme from her childhood.

"Ach, ich fühl's, es ist verschwunden, Ewig hin der Liebe Glück!"

Even though she sang of lost love, all she could think of was Bianca's sneaky little trick. She had some nerve stealing Alaina's dress. What had Alaina ever done to her? Sure, she'd beaten her in a few competitions back in their Julliard days, but that was a long time ago, and fair was fair. It wasn't her fault Bianca was such a sore loser.

Altez stopped the orchestra and Alaina's voice trailed off.

"No, no, no." He gestured to Alaina. "You're sounding too *agitato*, too irritated. Pamina isn't pissed at Tamino, she's lamenting over the loss of his love."

Alaina nodded as shame burned in her cheeks. She'd let Bianca get the better of her. It was ruining her performance just like Bianca wanted. She'd played right into her hand.

"Got it." Alaina nodded, secretly cursing herself. She could do better than this.

Altez raised his baton. "Again, from the beginning."

As the strings pulsed their heavy chords, Alaina tried to put herself in the mind set of someone who'd lost their true love. She thought of all of her own disappointments, starting with high school and going right through to the Italian tour last summer, when that oboe player stole the hottie tour guide she'd wanted. But, none of them were love. Not true love.

Alain realized on stage, in that moment, she'd never experienced true love at all. Only when she had, could she sing this aria in the way it was supposed to be sung. The Elizabeth Taylor look-a-like at her audition had been right. She'd never rise to the aria's power unless she had experiences of her own. Could Lance change that?

CHAPTER ELEVEN

Work and Play

Brett gathered his courage and picked up the old plastic phone in his apartment. Alaina's card rested in his other hand, her alluring picture smiling at him like she had some great secret to tell. It was embarrassing enough he'd waited this long. But he'd to make sure his phone number was private so it wouldn't register on Alaina's cell in case she tracked it back to his shitty apartment. The phone company hadn't called back until this afternoon, and he'd been out on the job all day.

He dialed the number. Hopefully, she'd still pick up.

The phone rang twice. "Hello?" Her velvety voice sang across the other end.

"Alaina?"

"Yes. Who do I have the pleasure of talking with?" She teased as though she smiled when she said it. He could picture that smile right down to the red lipstick. He'd tasted that lipstick and those lips.

"It's…Lance." God did he wish he could say his real name.

"Lance! I was beginning to think you had second thoughts."

Speak like a businessman, not like some backwoods logger. "My apologies. I had some…issues to attend to."

"Well, I hope you got them straightened out."

"I did." Most of them, anyway. There was still the massive elephant in the room called Lance.

"So, we're still on for this weekend?"

"Absolutely." He couldn't wait. Every shift finished meant he was another day closer to seeing her.

"Good, because I bought my hiking shoes. I'm looking forward to breaking them in."

He bet she looked great in them. Alaina could make a potato chip bag look sexy. "I can't wait to see them."

"And you already have yours, I take it?"

"Of course. Wouldn't leave home without them." Brett had a pair his father had given him when he'd started working at their logging company. They were well worn in, but he couldn't bring himself to throw them out and upgrade.

"Should I pick you up Friday night, let's say around five?"

"Sure." Brett would have to get out of work early, but Phil would cover for him. After securing a date with Sarah due to Brett's blunt tactics, Phil owed him one.

"Okay, I'll meet you at your office."

"No!" Panic surged inside him. "I may not be there at that time." *Think, think, think…* Why don't we meet at the Met? I've always wanted to take a tour."

"You've never been to a performance there?" She sounded surprised.

Brett cursed silently. A Wall Street businessman would have visited at least once. He didn't want her thinking he severely lacked culture. But, the closest thing he'd seen to opera was the commercial with the singers riding the bus. Oh, and that Bugs Bunny cartoon in his childhood where Bugs cuts Elmer Fudd's hair. Did that count? "I'm afraid I haven't had the time."

He bit his tongue.

"How tragic. Well, you'll have to come to mine. It's next

weekend. I can get you a free ticket. Although, you can probably afford your own."

"No, a free ticket would be nice. Especially if it comes from you."

"Aren't you sweet." Alaina sighed. "I'll stop by the box office before Friday."

"Thanks. I'd love to hear you sing." Man, this woman was aggressive, she'd asked him out three times, and he hadn't even said a thing. Sure took the pressure off his shoulders. Maybe all these years he'd been missing out by dating shy girls who couldn't say boo to a tree.

"And you shall. But not this weekend." Alaina laughed. "All work and no play makes me crazy."

He laughed, deciding to give her some of her own medicine. He couldn't keep the lust from his voice. "Don't worry. We'll play."

***

Alaina hung up the phone feeling hot all over. Had she finally met her match? Lance drove her crazy in both good and bad ways. She'd waited forever into eternity for his call, but when he had called, he didn't disappoint. Could she put up with his mysterious absences on a long-term basis? She'd never dated a Wall Street businessman before, so maybe his busy life was part of the package.

She turned off the lights and climbed underneath her satin bed sheets. Sleep came easily now that she taught at the school during the day and sang in her rehearsals at night. The twelve-hour days gave her a sense of accomplishment. She never thought helping others would bring her so much joy.

Alaina closed her eyes and breathed deeply. Her last thoughts were of Lance's rugged face.

"Dolce, *it has to be more* dolce." *Altez pleaded with Alaina from his conductor's podium in front of the orchestra. He tapped his baton insistently and the violinists picked up their bows. "Again. From the beginning."*

"You don't have what it takes." Bianca whispered from backstage. She wore a pink mini dress three sizes smaller than Alaina could squeeze into, with matching pink heels. "You can't even fit in your wardrobe."

Alaina looked down in horror. She wore nothing but a towel, and her hair dripped water on stage. How could she have come so ill prepared?

The orchestra began to play, but she didn't recognize any of the music. Panic surged inside her, constricting her throat. What scene were they in?

She pulled on Tamino's arm and he turned around. He was dressed in a black coat with a white scarf around his neck- not the traditional princely garb he'd worn at the other rehearsals. He started signing, "Dalla Sua Pace..."

That wasn't The Magic Flute. He'd sung the first aria of Don Giovanni.

She ran backstage, clutching the towel. There must be some mistake. She must have come on the wrong day or the wrong time. Alaina found the costume rack and dug for something more appropriate. She pulled out a tiny ballerina's tutu, then a slender long gown that would have fitted her left leg. Next, a clown's costume made for a ten year old. Every outfit she picked was too small.

Where was Catherine? Wasn't she supposed to fix her gown?

Her phone rang. Alaina followed the chime of Beethoven's fifth symphony to the audience and found her purse. The number was private.

Lance! It had to be him. Maybe he could help her- bring her something more fitting to wear. She pressed the receive button and held it up to her ear. "Hello?"

Silence, then static.

Alaina raised her voice. "Hello? Lance?"

Mrs. DeBarr's voice came on the other line. "You can't have him. He doesn't belong to you."

"Excuse me, ma'am. I just want to take him out for the weekend.

I'll bring him back."

"Nonsense!" Mrs. DeBarr growled. "You don't know what true love is."

Alaina dropped the phone. Mrs. DeBarr was right. She didn't know, and Altez could hear it in her voice. She'd only fool them for so long.

Alaina shot up in bed, anxiety eating a hole in her stomach. What a dream. It had played upon all her insecurities, her size, her singing, her inexperience with true love. Could Altez hear her fear in her voice? She certainly hoped not.

Hazy morning sunlight filtered through the beige curtains of her high-rise apartment. Alaina checked the alarm. Five more minutes until it went off. She could have used those extra minutes of sleep, but not if she had to stay in that awful dream. Instead of lying back down, she pulled herself out of bed and started the shower. Two more days and then Lance would be all hers for the weekend. She could make it through.

When she got to class, most of the students sat at their desks with their heads down, scribbling. She looked over a few shoulders of the kids in the back and pride surged through her.

They were writing their operas.

"What are we doing today, Ms. Amaldi?" John pulled back his greasy hair and actually made eye contact. He still wore the same sweatshirt he'd worn all last week. Alaina made a note to go out and buy him a few more over the weekend with Lance. She bet the lodge had some nice ones.

"Today we're writing the themes."

"You mean actual music?" Jackie narrowed her eyes.

"That's right." Alaina walked to the front of class. "I've brought some mp3s from Wagner's famous opera Tristan and Isolde. He uses the same thematic organization that John Williams does in Star Wars. Every character has a theme."

Jackie raised her hand. This time her long sleeves were tight, covering her wrists. Alaina hoped the scars weren't any worse. She'd reported Jackie's scars to the school nurse, but the overworked woman had insisted the school had already talked to her mom. Wondering if she'd ever get close enough to Jackie to ask about it herself, Alaina nodded to the girl. "Yes?"

"How are we supposed to write music if we don't know what it sounds like?"

She had a point. They didn't have keyboards or notation programs. All she had was a stack of staff paper. "I'll sing it for you." She handed out the paper, each student taking a sheet and passing down the rest. "Think of the intervals. You all took Music Theory One. You know what each interval sounds like. Put them together to develop a theme that fits each character."

She played them the Tristan and Isolde excerpts, and they began composing their own themes. She knew none of them had enough harmony experience to write an entire orchestral score, but she was taking this one step at a time and making it up as she went along. It could be a total disaster, but at least they all were having fun and learning.

After class, Jackie showed up for her first vocal lesson.

"You sure you want to do this?" Jackie placed her backpack on the floor and gave her a practiced look of defiance mixed with disappointment as though she wasn't worth the extra time.

"Of course!" Alaina threw up her arms. "You're very talented, and with some coaching you could go really far. Now, the change isn't going to be right away, and you have to be willing to practice." She raised both eyebrows.

Jackie shrugged and played with the frayed end of her sleeve. "Yeah, I'll practice."

"Okay, good. We're going to start with a few warm up exercises." Alaina straightened her posture and they started to sing together. Jackie was a fast learner, and she copied Alaina's voice right down to the vibrato width and speed.

Alaina checked the time, wanting to stay, but she had rehearsal in thirty minutes, and she didn't want to cut it as close as last time. "Work on those exercises and I'll see you next week for your next lesson, okay?"

Jackie nodded. She picked up her backpack and walked to the door. As Alaina packed up, the girl turned back around. "Why are you doing this?" Suspicion weighed her voice, as though she thought Alaina was dishing out pity lessons to fulfill some sort of volunteer obligation.

Guilt pricked the hairs on Alaina's neck. She had started this job because Altez had forced her to, but now she enjoyed it. These lessons were not part of her original contract. She'd decided to put in the extra time on her own.

Alaina met her gaze. "Because I believe in you."

CHAPTER TWELVE

Pearl

Brett stood on the steps of the Met feeling as though he'd shed his disguise. Dressed in a brown pull over sweater and jeans, he looked more like his true self and less like the man he was supposed to be. What else would you wear to a mountain lodge? Certainly not the tux that lay in the garment bag across his suitcase on the sidewalk- another gift from Mrs. DeBarr. He'd brought it just in case they went to a formal dinner.

"Lance DeBarr? I almost didn't recognize you."

Brett turned around and silently cursed. Bianca stood a step above him smiling like she'd caught him with his pants down. Maybe meeting at the Met was a bad idea.

She looked him up and down. "You certainly didn't come from the office."

"I had today off." Why did she look so suspicious? Had she overheard his conversation by the elevator? Or seen him on the construction site? As much as he tried to convince himself otherwise, she still reminded him of a cat with a mouse between its paws.

"You lucky man." She stepped down to the same level. "What brings you to my neck of the woods?"

Ironically, there were no "woods" to speak of anywhere near the building. "I'm meeting Alaina."

A sour look passed her face before she wiped it off. "Oh how sweet. Are you two going on another date?"

That was none of her business. But, the truth might shoe her away. "As a matter of fact, we are."

Another sour look crossed her face, this one even worse, like she'd drunk sewage water. "What did she have to pay this time?"

"Absolutely nothing at all." Alaina climbed the steps to meet them. She looked stunning in black skinny jeans and a red blazer the color of her hair. She reached Brett and threaded her arm through his. The faint scent of roses aroused his senses.

Brett breathed in relief, although standing between the two of them wasn't much better then standing alone with Bianca. The air turned tense as they shot daggers at one another with their eyes.

"I didn't think we had a rehearsal today." Alaina gave Bianca a suspicious look.

Bianca put her hand on her hip. "We didn't. I was just meeting with a few members of the cast to go over some harmonies."

Alaina tensed, her grip squeezing Brett's arm. "I wasn't invited."

"I know." Bianca smiled. "We didn't need you. Besides, aren't you doing charity work during the day, blessing kids with your presence?"

"I teach them music." Alaina's voice had a growly edge to it.

"I bet you do." Bianca turned to Brett. "I'm thinking of investing some money in the stock market, and I know you'd be the best person to turn to. Let me know when you have some free time."

Brett resisted the urge to squirm. "I'm sure I can help you sometime."

"Good." Bianca started down the steps. "You two have fun."

Once she was out of earshot, Brett turned to Alaina. "For a minute there, I thought she was coming with us!"

Alaina laughed. "Not in a million years."

Below them, Bianca got into a cab and drove off. Brett wasn't sorry to see her leave, and he wasn't the only one. "What's the problem between you two?"

Alaina winced. "You noticed?"

"It's hard not to."

She sighed. "Honestly, I have no idea. She didn't seem to like me from the start. Back in our Julliard days, I beat her in a few singing competitions and I guess she never got over it. She didn't think I deserved to win."

"Why not?"

Alaina shrugged, looking sexy in her red blazer as the wind played with strands of her hair. "Because I was rich and had everything she wanted? I don't know."

"You should talk to her about it." Brett couldn't help but step in. People always danced in circles around the truth, and it drove him nuts. Why not just say what you're thinking and be done with it?

Thick, sticky guilt rolled over him. *Take some of your own advice, man.*

Alaina glanced away toward where Bianca's cab had disappeared. "I'd never thought of that. Do you always take the straightforward approach?"

He scratched his head, feeling like the biggest hypocrite to ever walk those steps. "I try." If only he could in this case. But, if he did, would he be standing here taking a tour of the opera house, or would she have passed him by on the street without a second look?

He changed the subject. "You look lovely."

"Thanks. You're looking very outdoorsy. I like it."

"More than the tux?"

Alaina sucked her lower lip as she thought about her answer. She nodded slowly, examining him as though he were a fine painting. "I think I do. For some reason, this look seems more natural to you. You're less tense."

"Good." A ray of hope shone through his heart. That's what he normally looked like. Maybe she'd like the real him after all.

They walked into the lobby. The decorations from the cocktail

100

party had been taken down, but the place didn't seem any less grand. The chandeliers dangled above them in golden starbursts of light, and the red carpets reminded him of the glamor of Hollywood. How she could get up on stage and sing her heart out in a place like this, he had no idea. Alaina had guts.

"This you've already seen." She smiled as if thinking back to their first meeting.

He nodded. How could he forget? He'd met her over by the red carpeted staircase. Never had tea sounded so good.

"But what you haven't seen is the best part." She took his arm and led him into the main theater.

Brett craned his neck, surrounded by balcony after balcony of red seats separated by gold railings. He had the same feeling of vastness that came over him when he stood at the bottom of a great valley, looking up at the highest mountain peaks. The majesty made him feel small in a good way, like there was more to life than paving sidewalks.

Alaina twirled around and spread her arms. Her love for the opera house shone in her sparkling green eyes. It was like seeing someone inside their dream. "It contains three thousand eight hundred seats and one hundred and seventy-five standing room places."

"Very impressive." Brett rested his hand on the top of one of the seats. "Have you always wanted to sing here?"

"Have I wanted anything else?" She walked down the rows of chairs toward the stage. I first sat in this audience when I was twelve. My parents took me to see The Marriage of Figaro." She pointed up to the farthest balcony. "We sat all the way up there."

Brett moved closer to her and leaned in, trying to see where she pointed to. "Must have made quite an impression."

Alaina's gaze grew distant, as if she was thinking back. "One of the sopranos stood beneath me on the edge of the stage wearing a beautiful gown in the style of the eighteenth century- you know the ones with the frilly sleeves?"

Brett shrugged. He was not an expert on *any* women's apparel in *any* century.

"Anyway, her voice was so strong and so pure. It called to me like nothing else had. I felt the pain and joy even though I didn't understand the words. I wanted to *be* her, standing on that stage and giving people the experience of the story."

Brett pictured the little girl Alaina in the balcony, dreaming about the future. He pulled her toward him, impressed she saw her dream all the way through. "And here you are today."

Alaina glanced away, suddenly shy. "I had a lot of help from my parents and my teachers."

"Yes, but it's you that has to stand up there and sing." He laughed to himself. "I'd rather crawl in sewage water than sing in public. It takes guts."

Alaina ran her finger down his cheek to his chin. "It takes guts to work in the stock market. Give me music over numbers any day."

Brett pulled away. She admired him for something he didn't even do. If only he could tell her the truth. Every time he lied, a dagger stuck deeper into his gut.

Alaina followed him. "Are you living your dream as well?"

He turned and froze. This time he would tell her the truth, even if it didn't fit in his Lance persona. He braced himself on a seat, placing both hands on the rim. "I was until the fire took everything away."

Compassion crossed her beautiful face. "You mean the cabin in the woods?"

Brett nodded, agony crashing through him as he tightened his grip.

She touched his arm. "I'm so sorry."

He shrugged, pushing away the pain threatening to overwhelm him. Why had he brought this up? "What's done is done."

Alaina stepped toward him and caught his gaze. "You should build another cabin." She spoke with such certainty, as though it were the only way to heal.

"I hadn't thought of that before." He couldn't bring his parents back. But, could he rebuild in their memory? What good would it do? The cabin would never have his mother's embroidery on the windowsills, or his father's wood sculptures on the walls.

"I could help you." She smiled sheepishly, looking too cute for him to be angry at her suggestion. "If you need it, of course. I don't know much about architecture, but I could help design the inside."

Brett imagined building another cabin, this time with Alaina's help. It was a ridiculous offer. They hardly knew each other, yet here she was looking like she meant every word of it.

He tried to wrap his mind around the idea. Build another cabin? Nothing could recapture what he'd had. But that didn't mean he couldn't find another home with someone else. Maybe. Even though a year had gone by, the ache was still raw in his heart. When he dug deeper, a sliver of hope glimmered there as well, like a pearl that had survived the fire; one single white orb in dark ash and soot.

He met Alaina's gaze. "Someday I might take you up on your offer."

"I hope you do." She stared right back at him, unmoving. The air between them thickened with unspoken promises.

The door to the theater opened behind them, and a young woman dressed as a flamingo jogged down the aisle.

Brett blinked in surprise. "What the…?"

"She's from the production." Alaina smiled and took his arm. "Come on, our limo is waiting."

***

Alaina buckled herself in and watched the mob of people walking on the sidewalk as the limo pulled away from the Met. Sightseers with cameras around their necks, businessmen in crisp suits, old ladies walking their white, fluffy dogs, and teenagers dressed in hoodies and frayed jeans hurried down the street. So many people, and in this chaotic mess she'd found Lance.

He'd grown silent after their conversation about his cabin. He'd opened up more than he'd done on their first date, and she'd finally learned a kernel of truth about the real Lance. Something about that cabin claimed his heart, and if she wanted to be in there somewhere, than she'd have to find out what exactly it was.

But not right now. She'd pressed a little too far when she'd offered to help him build a new cabin. The words had flown from her mouth without thought, straight from her heart. All she'd wanted to do was help him, but you can't always replace something lost with a shiny brand new one.

When she was seven, her cat, Issy became sick, and her father had to take him to the vet to 'go to sleep.' She'd said goodbye, kissing his furry head with tears running down her cheeks. She couldn't eat anything the whole day, and at night, she stared at his empty bed, some of his hairs still there.

The next week, her dad brought home a tiny kitten with the same mottled brown and black hair. At first, she hated it. That kitten couldn't replace Issy. She wouldn't let it sleep in Issy's bed, and her parents had to buy a new one. It took Alaina months to grow to love it in a different way.

That was exactly what she'd done to Lance. She'd offered him a replacement kitten. He seemed to take it better than she had at seven years old, but still, she could see the battle clashing in his stormy dark eyes.

And his suggestion about talking with Bianca? That had smacked her right in the face. She'd never thought of confronting her. But, the idea grew on her the more she considered it. Lance wasn't the type of guy to dance around issues. He didn't waste time, and he got things done. Maybe that's what she needed to do with Bianca to put a stop to her sabotage.

"Have you ever been to northern New Hampshire?" Lance had shifted in his seat so his back was turned toward the window and his full attention fell on her.

"No. It's not exactly a bustling cultural center."

He laughed. "Is that your prerogative for visiting cities?"

"It was." She made a point to sound serious. "I think I've been a little bit of a snob. But I'm realizing there's more to a place than its opera house. I like trying new things with you."

"I like that." He smiled for the first time since he'd seen her on the steps. "It means a lot to me."

"Me, too." Alaina reached across the seat and placed her hand over his. This guy was too good to be true. Not only was he sexy, smart, and laid back, he also spoke his mind. Besides his butt, she liked his blunt honesty the most.

The scenery changed from paved city streets to endless forest stretching out in all directions. Gold, red, burnt amber, and yellow leaves caught the rays of the setting sun. It was hard to think that the serenity of these places existed just hours outside of the bustle of New York.

When they reached New Hampshire, they passed quaint towns with white chapels, golden fields and classic old barns. A year ago, she'd thumb her nose at a drive through Nowhere-Ville. But, now, she couldn't think of being anywhere else.

The limo pulled off the highway for gas and they drove by a few old, colonial homes with covered porches and shuttered windows. Red wood peeked through the foliage. At first she thought it was another barn, but the wood hung suspended above thin air.

"Is that a covered bridge?" Alaina pointed out the window as the limo pulled up to a gas station.

"It is." Lance unbuckled his seat belt. "Come on, let's check it out."

Before she could protest, he'd circled the vehicle and opened her door.

Alaina stepped out hesitantly. "But, I don't think the driver means to be here long."

Lance took her hand. "Trust me. He won't leave without us."

Hand in hand, they jogged across the main road to a smaller

dirt road leading to the bridge. A brook weaved through a valley, separating a copse of trees from a field with a rusting, antique Chevrolet covered in yellow leaves.

Just hours ago, she stood on the steps of the Met, and now here she was in the middle of nowhere, on a covered bridge with Lance.

Wooden beams crisscrossed above them as their steps echoed on the suspended wood. The planks were uneven, each one beautiful in a unique way with the swirly patterns of the aging wood. Nail heads as thick as quarters held the planks together.

Lance walked to the middle of the bridge and spread his arms. "What do you think?"

She shook her head, feeling as though she finally noticed and appreciated things that surrounded her all her life. "I can't believe I never thought to leave the city and go exploring. I guess I didn't think it was worth my time."

Lance's face grew serious. "And is it now?"

She walked toward the edge and gazed out the crisscrossing weave work where the brook trailed off in the distance. She ran her fingertips over the rough wood. "I always felt like the city was everything. If you wanted to be someone, then that's where you had to stay. If I left New York, even for a few days, all my hard work and sacrifice would slip through my fingers."

She turned back to Lance. The fading sunset trickling through the cracks in the wood brought out the chestnut highlights in his dark hair. He looked gorgeous.

The truth hit Alaina in the gut. "Right now I can't think of being anywhere else."

Lance closed the distance between them in three bold steps. He placed his hand under her chin and brought his face down to hers. He kissed her without hesitation, his lips pressed firmly against hers in unabashed passion.

Alaina kissed him back, smoothing her hands around the back of his head and his neck. His boldness awakened desire deep within her. She loved a man who knew what he wanted, and he made her feel like no man had ever wanted her more.

He pulled back and gasped for breath before kissing her again and again on her top lip, her bottom lip, the side of her mouth.

Want surged inside her. She needed to be closer. They had too many layers of clothes.

"Ah-hem."

They broke the kiss, turning toward the opening of the bridge. The limo driver stood with his hands on his hips, an admonishing look on his face.

Alaina cringed back, embarrassed. Her own driver would have waited patiently by the limo. Firing him back in Italy was the worst decision she'd ever made.

The driver checked his watch. "I take it you want to reach the hotel by nightfall?"

"Of course." Lance threaded his arm through hers. He turned toward her as if they'd just ended a pleasant conversation. "Shall we?"

Alaina nodded as her cheeks burned. She felt like she was in high school all over again. Since when did limo drivers act as chaperones?

Since they were paid for the trip and not by the hour. When she got back, she'd have to call her old driver and apologize.

As they walked back to the limo, she waited until the driver was out of earshot and slapped Lance on the arm. "You brought me here to steal a kiss."

Lance laughed and stared at her hungrily. "It's not stealing if you want it, too."

CHAPTER THIRTEEN

Bumps in the Night

Excitement rose in Brett's chest as the limo crested the ridge and the White Mountain Lodge stood out among the pines like a wooden fort perched on the top of a foothill. Four red roofed turrets surrounded the six storey structure. Red flags waved in the breeze.

As they rode nearer, he could make out rows and rows of shuttered windows and a two storey covered porch stretching around the foundation. Giant beams, as thick as trees, held up the porch at even intervals, each one decorated with hanging baskets of wildflowers. The resort had the elegance of the White House merged with the rustic backdrop of the mountain.

He loved every inch of it.

Alaina pointed to a sign. "Look, its Oktoberfest this month. The sign says they have a haunted hayride, a ghost hunt, and a resident medium giving workshops." She raised an eyebrow. "Are you frightened by ghosts?"

Oh no, she had an overactive imagination- which could be good and bad. Brett gave her an exasperated look. "I don't believe in them."

"You might after this weekend." She wiggled her finger. "Let's see if I can get you scared."

"Want to wager?" Brett raised an eyebrow. There was no way she could so much as worry him. He'd grown up in the woods, and he'd grown accustomed to the rustling of leaves in the wind and the trees creaking at night. The scariest thing he'd ever seen was Bianca walking through his construction site.

"Yeah, I'll bet one kiss you'll be spooked by the end of the weekend."

"One kiss?" That sounded like she had more to gain than loose. Boy did Alaina know how to use any topic to flirt. He liked that. "And what if you win?"

"Then you'll be the one doing the kissing."

If it was anything like back on the covered bridge, they'd both kiss each other, but who was he to argue? "Done."

"Good." Alaina leaned over and spoke in a hushed tone. "You should come with me sometime to my grandparents' house in Syracuse. Built in the eighteen hundreds; every room seems alive. You don't even want to go to the bathroom alone in that place."

Brett smiled. "Is this another invitation for another date?"

Alaina shrugged. "Maybe."

He stretched his arms and yawned as if bored. "If you're trying to scare me with ghost stories from grandma's house, you've got your work cut out for you."

"And if you're trying to act all macho, like nothing will scare you, then you've got something coming and you're not gonna like it."

He shrugged. "I don't know. I think I'll like it a lot."

She slapped him. "Watch your mouth."

He rubbed his arm where she'd hit him and smiled. "With you around, I should be watching my back."

They carried their bags into a grand foyer. A giant, bearskin rug covered a polished hardwood floor. Tapestries of woodland scenes hung from the walls beside a massive stone fireplace roaring with flames.

They checked in and hauled their luggage up two flights of

stairs to a room overlooking the foothills of the mountain in a misty green landscape. One enormous bed covered in furs stood at the other end.

Desire rose inside him, along with apprehension. "One bed?"

Alaina winked. "We're all adults here." She set her bags down on a velvet padded bench by two dressers. "But, if you prefer, I can go back down and-"

"No, this will be fine." He didn't want Alaina assuming he didn't want her or that he was some strange, private man who couldn't share a room with a pretty lady. But, she didn't even know his true identity. He couldn't go any farther with her while pretending to be Lance. It wouldn't be honorable. Besides that, he still couldn't get over the fact that she was just too good for him; like a goddess to a servant.

"What do you think?" She strutted across the room, her long, shapely legs showing off a mean pair of red hiking boots, matching her blazer and her hair.

Brett blinked in surprise. "You look magnificent."

"Well, I don't know about *magnificent*." She laughed and grabbed his arm. "You might want to save that one for my Pamina gown- after Catherine fixes it."

"Pamina?" Was he missing something?

"She's the character I play in the opera." A suspicious look crossed her face. "Haven't you ever seen *The Magic Flute* before?"

Uh oh. The magic what? His chest tightened. Should he know? "Remind me."

"It's the opera I'm getting you tickets for."

"Of course." As soon as he got back, he'd look it up on Phil's phone. By the time of the performance, he'd be an expert. He hated having to hide his classical music delinquency, but Lance DeBarr wouldn't have such a hole in his music history knowledge and he had to keep up the snobby appearance, at least until Mrs. DeBarr found enough money to fund her research to save her husband.

Alaina tugged on his sleeve. "Come on, if we go to the tavern for dinner, we don't have to dress up."

"I brought my tux just in case." He gestured backwards as they left the room.

"I see that." She slipped the key in her pocket. "But, what good will that do on our haunted hayride?"

"You mean we're going tonight?"

"Mmhmm." She squeezed his arm. "Prepare to be scared."

Brett shook his head in resignation. "Oh I'm prepared all right." Prepared to laugh.

After a dinner of roasted butternut squash, glazed chicken, and pumpkin pie, they walked out back to the barn where a middle-aged man harnessed four Clydesdale horses to a wagon which was full of hay.

"Take a seat. My name's Elmer, and I'll be your guide for the night."

He gestured toward the wagon. Another young couple already sat inside.

The sun had set, and stars twinkled in the sky overhead. Pretty soon, it would be pitch black. Brett glanced at Alaina. "You sure you want to do this?"

She narrowed her eyes as she petted the lead horse. "Are you sure?"

He nodded in exasperation. There was no playing chicken with her.

Brett helped her into the wagon and they sat opposite the other couple. Felt blankets were folded in the corner, and he grabbed one and laid it out over their legs. Alaina nestled against him, hugging his arm.

This was perfect. The outdoors, the smell of the hay mixed with her rosy scent, her glowing, auburn hair cascading down his shoulder. He couldn't ask for more. Well, maybe for her to know his true name and identity, but that would have to wait until another day.

The driver gave the horses a command and they started down

a long trail leading into the woods. Alaina held onto him through the bumps, and he settled into the rocking of the wagon, feeling the crisp night air on his skin and their combined warmth under the blanket. He was thankful for the other couple's presence- they kept him from getting too far. If it was only him and Alaina under that felt blanket, it would be difficult to restrain himself.

The only light came from two hanging lanterns on either side of the driver. He turned his head back toward them, trusting the horses to lead them forward on the path. "Have any of you heard the ghost tale of the White Mountain Lodge?"

Both Brett and Alaina shook their heads, as did the other couple. Brett resisted the urge to roll his eyes. *Great, here we go.*

Elmer paused, as though thinking how to start. "The man who owned this property was Sterling White. He inherited the land from his father, Casper White, a successful oil tycoon. You know- rich as can be- the kind of man who shined his shoes with hundred dollar bills. Anyhow, so he gave his son this land, and his son decided to build a great estate in honor of his new fiancé, Hilda Sweeten. So he and Hilda get married in the lobby, right in front of the old stone fireplace way back in…"

He counted on his fingers, "Nineteen oh two."

Alaina glanced at Brett and smiled. Did she believe this crap?

Elmer checked on the horses, then turned back to them. "So they get married, and everything's going well until she comes down with this fever and gets real sick."

His tone turned solemn. "Sterling has all the doctors in the county come up and treat her. But nothing's helping. The last quack suggests she get some fresh air, so they carry her outside and up this small foothill where she can see the mountain. In fact, I think they took this very trail."

"Oh no, not this trail." Alaina whispered in amusement.

Brett shushed her. "Let Elmer tell the story."

Elmer gave them an admonishing look. "So, she asks for water, and the doc and Sterling go down to the brook, just a few feet from this very spot. When they carry the pitcher up to her, she's gone."

He paused. Brett assumed it was for effect. This guy was good. Must have a lot of practice with these hayrides.

Concern crossed the face of the woman across from them. "Did they find her?"

Yup. Played right into his hand.

Elmer's voice dropped low. "So they look all around the area, organizing search parties and what say you. But, they never find her. Some say she'd only pretended to be sick- that Sterling was holding her captive and this was her only chance to get away. Others say she wandered off a cliff or met a huge, black bear and her remains are still here somewhere. They say her spirit walks these woods at night, her nightgown all muddied and frayed, and her face dripping sweat from the fever, looking for her way home."

"Often, tourists see a woman in a nightgown crossing the trail. They say once you get too close, the fever comes over you, and you're sick for days. I, myself, only saw her once, many years ago when I was hiking in these woods. Saw her just over there, by that old pine, standing behind the tree and weeping, her hands covering her eyes."

Elmer turned back to the trail. "Hold it just a sec. I see a fire up ahead." He brought in the reins and the horses stopped. Without the creaking of the wagon, the silence felt empty.

He gave them a wicked grin. "Be right back."

Elmer left the reins in his seat and jumped off the wagon. He disappeared down the trail.

Alaina glanced over the horses. "I don't see a fire."

The other couple shifted uncomfortably. The woman shivered. "Is he just going to leave us here?"

"I'm sure he'll come back, hon." He husband smoothed her hair.

Alaina turned to Brett. "What do you think about that story?"

Brett shrugged. For some reason it reminded him of Mrs. DeBarr. The part about Sterling seeking every doctor in the area, and having them all fail was like Mrs. DeBarr trying to find a cure for her husband. The likeness made the hair on the back of his neck rise up. But, it didn't mean there were ghosts out there in the woods.

One of the horses neighed. Another tapped his hoof on the ground.

"The horses are getting skittish." Alaina didn't realize how hard she gripped his arm.

Brett smiled to himself. This was all part of the White Mountain Lodge's plan. He was sure of it. Elmer told the story with just the right timing to end here and leave the wagon. Pretty soon, something was going to jump out at them. Maybe even Elmer himself.

Should he tell Alaina?

Watching her fret over the horses was too much fun. Maybe it was better she got a taste of her own medicine. She was the one who wanted to come on this crazy hayride in the dark- to scare *him*.

The other couple glanced with worry over the edge of the wagon.

"What if he doesn't come back?" The wife pulled the blanket up to her chin.

"Then we walk back." The husband patted her hand. "We couldn't have traveled far."

A branch cracked in the woods beside them and Alaina jerked up. "What was that?"

Was that fear in her eyes? Guilt rolled over him. He should at least give her a clue about the prank, but he didn't want to spoil it for the other couple.

A low deep moan echoed through the woods. Alaina clung to his arm, her fingernails digging in.

Brett sighed. "It's probably just-"

"Look over there!" The woman across from them pointed at a figure about seven feet from the wagon.

Brett had to give Elmer credit. The lady standing in the woods in the muddied and tattered white nightgown looked pretty darn real. She approached them slowly, her arms outstretched.

Gimme a break.

114

Alaina jumped to her feet. "We have to get out of here."

Brett scrambled to hold her down, but she wiggled out of his grasp. She grabbed his arm and tried to pull him up. "I'm not leaving you here."

At least he knew if there was a catastrophe, she'd take the time to rescue him. He burst out in laughter.

Alaina stared at him like he was crazy. Then, the other couple started to laugh as well. She glanced around wildly. "What the...?"

Hilda's ghost stopped a few feet from the carriage and put her arms down. At this distance, the white make-up of her pale complexion was obvious. Elmer stood in front, leaning on a tree.

The ghost smiled, looking more like a girl in a costume. "Welcome to the Haunted Hayride."

Surprise, then anger flashed on Alaina's face. "You!" She slapped Brett's arm. "You knew all along!"

Brett couldn't stop laughing. An enormous sense of freedom and released trickled through him. He couldn't remember the last time he'd had so much fun.

Alaina pulled away and sat in the corner of the carriage shooting daggers at him with her eyes.

He reached over and grabbed her hand. "Come on. Please forgive me. I didn't want to spoil the surprise."

She snapped her hand away. "You wanted to see me freak out." She looked so sexy when she was mad. He resisted the urge to smile.

Brett raised both hands in defeat. "You're the one trying to scare me."

Elmer whipped the reins, and the horses turned around a bend and headed back for the hotel. Brett gave her space, hoping she'd come around. It wasn't like he'd planned the whole thing.

The other couple chatted up a storm across the wagon naming all the scary movies they'd seen as kids. He checked their hands-yup. Two marriage rings. Maybe someday he'd take his wife on a haunted hayride.

After the fire, he'd stopped dating. If it wasn't for meeting Phil, he would have stopped living and become a zombie- walking to work and home every day in a grind. Imagining a future without his parents and their logging business had been disrespectful to their memory. How could he move on after such tragedy? Now, he could see a life without them and it was still worth living. Alaina gave him hope.

That's if she ever forgave him. Was she the type to hold a grudge?

The wagon pulled up to the front of the hotel, and Brett jumped down and offered his hand. She pursed her lips as if considering it, then slid her hand in his and allowed him to help her down.

"So I guess you're not mad anymore?" Brett led her behind the married couple, envious of the fact they were holding hands.

"Not as much." Alaina crossed her arms over her chest. "To tell you the truth, I would have done the same in your shoes."

"Aha." Brett raised a finger. "A trickster at heart."

"That's not such a surprise, is it?" She smirked. "But, I had no idea you had a sneaky side, too."

Too sneaky. Brett swallowed a load of guilt. He'd gotten so good at fibbing these past few days, he could have grown a Pinocchio nose the length of a pool net. He pointed to a bar at the end of the lobby. "Come on, I'll make it up to you with a drink."

He ordered a beer, and she ordered a lemon-flavored margarita the size of a dinner plate with salt along the rim.

"You gonna drink that whole thing?" He took a seat at the bar.

"Watch me." Alaina raised both eyebrows in a challenge. She tugged on his sweater. "How about we sit in front of the fireplace?"

Brett paused. He didn't like getting too close to fire these days. It wasn't fear keeping him back. He just didn't trust it.

"Please?" Alaina sipped her margarita. "We can stretch out our legs."

Brett reminded himself a fireplace was hardly a raging forest fire. If he was ever going to learn to move on, then he had to take the first steps, and with Alaina, he could do that. "Okay."

They walked to the fireplace in the center of the lobby and sat down on a giant leather couch.

"So this is it." Alaina glanced up at the fireplace.

"Is what?" Brett sipped his beer. It had a dark, frothy taste perfect for a cold, autumn night.

Imagination sparked in her eyes. "The place where Sterling married Hilda."

"Oh come on, don't tell me you still believe all that."

Alaina shrugged. "I'm sure there's some truth to it. I've always been a sucker for crazy stories. That's one reason why I love opera."

"What about your own story? Is it crazy?" Lance played with a lock of her silky hair.

She glanced up at him. "Bidding on a date with a mystery man, riding on a haunted hayride...you tell me."

He shrugged. "I hope it's crazy enough to keep you interested."

She threaded her hands through his. "You're the craziest thing in it."

They finished their drinks, and she cuddled up next to him on the couch. He watched the fire as he listened to her breaths grow deeper. Holding her made him complete. Sure, he was incredibly attracted to her, but he also enjoyed spending time with her. She was witty, sarcastic, alluring, bold- so different than the snobby diva he thought she might be. She challenged him in ways he needed to be challenged and comforted him with the truest of hopes.

Apprehension grew inside him and the fire heated his skin until sweat beaded on his forehead. The truth was, he was falling hard for this woman, and she didn't have a clue who he truly was.

CHAPTER FOURTEEN

Message

Alaina woke up groggily to a room filled with bright sunlight. Where was she?

The White Mountain Lodge.

The Hayride.

That monstrous margarita.

Lance.

She felt the other side of the bed. Damn. She'd never forgive herself if she'd been too drunk to remember the hottest night of her life. Her hands touched cold, unwrinkled sheets. Nope. She'd slept in this bed alone.

Disappointment trickled through her.

She sat up, scanning the room. Lance lay on the other side, sleeping on the love seat in a white T-shirt and blue boxers. His legs dangled off the end ridiculously. He must have carried her up from the fireplace and tucked her in. *How sweet.* He was such a gentleman.

Unfortunately, in this case, she wouldn't mind if he'd been a little bad and woken her up.

Not wanting to wake him, she pulled herself out of bed and

slipped into the shower. No reason for him to see her with make-up smeared across her face and knotted hair. Leave that to after they'd made crazy love together.

Which would happen, she'd make sure of it.

Alaina dressed in her new hiking clothes as Lance slept. One thing was for sure- it would take quite the alarm to wake him up. She pictured mornings sleeping in together, getting up late and making pancakes and coffee. She hadn't thought about such normal, everyday things with anyone. They'd never appealed to her. Maybe she just hadn't met the right guy. But then Lance had shown up at the auction, emanating rough masculinity which was something a lot of classical musicians lacked.

She leaned over him, "Lance. Time to wake up."

"Who?" He blinked and rubbed his eyes.

That was strange. "It's me, Alaina."

"Alaina." Recognition registered in his eyes. "What time is it?"

She smiled. "Time for breakfast. It closes in fifteen minutes."

"Oh." He sat up and studied her face. "You look lovely."

She loved a man who gave blunt compliments. "Thanks. The shower helped."

Lance stretched his arms. "A shower's exactly what I need. Do I have time?" He stood and dug out some clean clothes from his suitcase.

If only she could come and watch. "If it's quick. I'm not missing my pancakes for anything."

Lanced laughed. "I'll be faster than a speeding train."

She waved him away. "Ha ha superman, let's go."

As he jumped in the shower, she noticed his wallet had fallen out of the pants he'd hung on the back of a chair. *Better pick it up for him or he'll lose it.*

Temptation lingered in her fingertips as she felt the smooth leather. What was in there? Pictures of Mrs. DeBarr? A zillion credit cards? A forgotten picture of his ex?

Her conscience weighed heavily on her shoulders. She wouldn't want him going through her purse and finding old tissues or her make-up. She may be a diva at times, but Alaina was not a snoop.

She placed the wallet on the table. Only then did she notice the name inscribed on the back.

To Brett, All my love, Dad.

Brett? Who's that?

Did he steal someone else's wallet?

The bathroom door opened along with a wave of steam. Lance stepped out, looking like a Gillette shaver model, his face smooth and his hair slicked back. He smelled like fresh pine and mint, and she wanted to nuzzle up next to his neck and place kisses all over his freshly shaven face. She almost forgot about the strange name.

He wiped a spot of shaving cream off his chin with a towel. "What's wrong?"

"It's nothing." She glanced away, not wanting to ruin the sexy moment.

"No, what is it? You look like you've seen a ghost." He smiled. "Pun intended."

His easy humor made her feel more comfortable. "I saw your wallet on the floor, so I picked it up for you. I didn't want you to forget it."

He stiffened. "That's fine." Something strange in his posture made her push the issue.

"Why does it say Brett?"

His face slackened and he wiped the towel over it. When he brought it down again, he was composed and calm. "That's my middle name. That's what they called me growing up."

Lance Brett DeBarr? What an odd name. Sure, both names were nice by themselves. But together, it just didn't flow right. Mrs. DeBarr had an odd choice of rhythm. Alaina raised both eyebrows.

"What? You think it's ugly, don't you."

"I didn't say that." She grabbed his arm. What difference did it make if his middle name didn't fit well with his first name? He was sexy as hell. "Come on, we're don't want to miss breakfast."

120

They exited the room and she checked to make sure the door was locked. Lance followed her down the stairs. "What's your middle name?"

Alaina shrugged. "It's not important."

"Oh come on, Miss Judgmental. Let's have it."

A colorful buffet lay on three tables in the center of the room along with a basket of Danishes. Alaina's stomach gurgled. They found a seat next to the window with a great view of the valley. Fog from the upper foothills cascaded down the mountainside as the sun lit up the autumn leaves like fire below.

The waiter came and filled their mugs with steaming, black coffee. After he left, Lance stared in apprehension. "So?"

Alaina rolled her eyes, hoping he would have forgotten or been distracted by all the food. "Oh all right. I was named after my great grandmother."

"And...?" He drank his coffee black. Interesting. Manly.

"Bertha."

Lance chocked, almost spitting out his coffee.

Her neck and cheeks burned. "What? It's an old fashion name, that's all."

He smirked. "Okay, Alaina *Bertha* Amaldi." He lingered on her middle name as if it was a jewel.

"Oh stop it." She threw her napkin at him. As much as he teased her, she couldn't help but enjoy it.

After a plate full of scrambled eggs and two pancakes, they walked up to the atrium to the gallery of the resident psychic. Perched at the summit of the hotel, the room had a sprawling view of the mountain. Potted ferns sat at each window, reaching toward the sun. It was the perfect place to sit and read or relax.

"I hope she knows something about me." Alaina directed them to the front row. She'd always wanted to attend one of these galleries ever since she saw one on television. She was hitting a lot of things on her bucket list these days- singing at the Met, going on a haunted hayride, falling in love. Well, hopefully that last one.

She wasn't sure if she and Lance would pan out just yet. Especially if he kept sleeping on the love seat and calling her Bertha.

Lance pulled her back. "Let's not sit up front."

"Oh come on. Don't be such a skeptic." She grabbed his arm and pulled him forward. "Play along for me."

"All right." He followed her to the front row. The audience filled up behind them.

Lance leaned in to whisper in her ear. "Man, this lady is popular."

Alaina folded her hands in her lap, excitement and nervous anticipation building inside her. "Let's hope it's because she's good."

She wasn't sure what she was looking for: a prediction of an outstanding performance, how many kids she'd have, a message from…well, no one close to her had passed on. Her grandparents were still living. The closest family death was her great Aunt Matilda, but she'd only met her once at a reunion when she was three.

A middle aged woman with long white hair wearing a light blue sundress and sandals walked in front of the crowd. Instead of calling their attention, she brought a wooden flute to her lips and played a solemn melody. Everyone quieted and turned toward the front.

***

Still reeling from Alaina's discovery of his wallet, Brett couldn't concentrate on what the psychic was saying. Sure, he'd covered it up, but that had come too close, and he hated lying to her. When he got back, he'd have to settle things with Mrs. DeBarr.

The psychic turned in their direction and Alaina grabbed his hand and squeezed. The woman reminded him of someone who'd walked out of the seventies with her billowy sundress and free spirited frizzy white hair. Her eyes were a little too big and strikingly blue. She met his gaze, sending an unnerving jolt up his spine.

"The month of April is significant." The older woman placed

her hand near her head twice. "I have two older people here... April keeps coming back to me. Does anyone know someone whose birthdays or deaths were in that month?"

Brett shifted in his chair. Both of his parents were born in that month, almost exactly one year apart. His father was born on April seventh and his mother on April tenth. But that didn't mean anything. A lot of people were born in April.

The psychic touched her mouth with her fingers, moving them back and forth over her lips. "They died of smoke inhalation. I feel as though their deaths were sudden."

Brett's stomach hollowed out. He placed a hand over his gut. Was the room getting hot? His collar pressed against his Adam's apple, giving him the urge to choke.

"I also feel as though they died before their time." She glanced over them. "Anyone over here?"

Alaina shook her head, her brow furrowed in thought.

Pain crashed through Brett as sweat beaded on his forehead. He looked down, unable to meet the psychic's gaze. Even if she was right, he couldn't acknowledge it. Alaina couldn't know about his real parents, not when he was pretending Mrs. DeBarr was his mother.

Besides, this was ridiculous. He didn't believe in ghosts. It was a train of coincidences. Nothing more.

The older woman closed her eyes. "I have a clear message from them: *she's the one.*" She opened her eyes and scanned the crowd. "Does that mean anything to anyone?"

It meant something to Brett. His mother never approved of any girls he brought home. She always used to tell him she'd let him know when he brought the right one home.

Why now? Why would she come through this hippy psychic lady to tell him that? Was Alaina the one?

The walls pressed in on him; too many people in too small a space. They all stared at him, their eyes like lasers on his back. The room spun, and his breakfast churned in his stomach. He'd eaten too much and not gotten enough sleep. Brett covered his face with his hands.

Alaina whispered beside him, "Are you okay?"

"I need some air." If he didn't move, he'd throw up right into one of the potted plants. Brett stood and left the room. He pushed through the glass doors leading to the back porch and breathed with relief as the cool air of the mountain spread over him. Leaning on the railing, he tried to make sense of what just happened.

The moment in the atrium seemed surreal, as if he'd dreamt it. There was no way his parents could communicate with him. They were gone.

Alaina placed a hand on his arm. "Is everything all right?"

Guilt weighed on his shoulders. He wanted to tell her the truth so badly. "Yeah, I think I had too much to eat."

"Tell me about it." Alaina rubbed her stomach. She pulled up two wooden lawn chairs. "Here, sit down, you'll feel better."

Brett wasn't sure anything would make him feel better. His senses prickled all around him as if electric energy charged the air. Alaina had been right. He was spooked, but not in the way he would have thought. It wasn't fear of ghosts, it was the confrontation of everything that had torn him apart.

"I'm kinda glad you got us out of there." Alaina rolled her eyes. "For a psychic, she stinks. She didn't reveal anything about me, and she kept talking about two people who didn't even have a connection in the audience."

Brett dropped his gaze to his feet. How could he tell her the psychic was spot on? It would ruin everything Mrs. DeBarr worked toward.

Alaina leaned toward him. "Are you sure you're going to be okay?"

He nodded. "I just need time. That's all. Time and some fresh air."

"Like Hilda?" Amusement crossed Alaina's pretty face.

A smile crept into his lips. "This is way different than the situation with Hilda." Even at a time like this, she cheered him up.

Whether his mom spoke to him back in that room or not, one thing was certain.

Alaina *was* the right one.

CHAPTER FIFTEEN

Baring it All

"So how long is this hike?" Alaina retied her hiking boots in double knots. A charged sense of determination roared inside her. But, she didn't want to push it too far on her first hike. If Lance had to wait for her, or they couldn't make it and they had to go back she'd die of embarrassment.

"Five miles." Lance hefted their backpack with all of their supplies and their packed lunch. "It's a piece of cake."

Color had returned to his face. He was in his element in the woods, and a relaxed calm had come over him- just what she thought might happen. He'd worried her for a moment back in the hotel.

"For someone who's hiked his whole life."

Lance gave her an exasperated look- which was exactly what she'd been going for. She loved to tease him.

"For a beginner as well." He stopped and touched her cheek. "Trust me. You'll enjoy it, and I've heard wonderful things about the waterfall at the end."

He turned around and continued and Alaina had to push herself to keep up. She was rethinking her overly large breakfast and that second pancake. She stepped over a fallen log and lost her balance, bracing herself against a tree. She scraped her skin against the hard bark. "So it's worth it?"

Lance turned around and winked. "I'll make it worth it."

That quickened her pace.

They reached a place where the ground leveled, allowing her to catch her breath. The uphill climb had taken all of her energy, but now she actually had some breath left for conversation. "What got you into hiking?"

Lance pushed aside a branch, holding it back for her to pass. "I grew up in the woods."

"In your family's cabin?"

He nodded. "My earliest memory was playing with my dog, Granger." Lance smiled fondly. "He was a German shepherd mutt that my dad found one day savaging for scraps. We'd do everything together. We used to go on long walks in the woods, and he'd find interesting things for me to take home- things my mother didn't like."

"Oh really?" She bet Mrs. DeBarr didn't like a lot of things. For some reason, she couldn't imagine the old woman in a log cabin or the woods for that matter.

"Once Granger found a sick crow. I brought it home, and my mother yelled at me, 'those things have diseases.' But that was the last thing I was worried about. All I wanted to do was save the bird, and all she wanted to do was keep me safe." He grew suddenly quiet.

Alaina wondered if his mother was a touchy subject. She was about to change the subject when Lance continued.

"Granger passed away when I was twelve. Just fell asleep on the door mat and never woke up. We didn't know how old he was, but my guess was about fourteen- pretty old for a dog that size."

"I'm sorry." Alaina thought of Issy. "My cat died when I was young as well. I loved that cat more than anything in the world."

He stopped in his tracks and studied her face. "I bet you did."

127

She nodded, comforted by his certainty. She didn't have to explain herself to him like she did with her parents. "It took me a long time to come to terms with it."

Lance touched her hair. "That's because you loved him very much."

A complex emotion passed his face, as though he understood her too well and she touched a dark place in his heart. He turned and continued on the trail. "After Granger died, I went for a hike along all the trails we'd walked together. I thought it would be painful, but the forest comforted me. I had this feeling like he was still there with me. Now, whenever I come back, I feel like I'm visiting an old friend." He shook his head. "I can't explain it. All I know is that the forest helped me heal, and after that, I always came back to it when I had something to work out."

Alaina followed him, honored he was opening up to her. She loved hearing anything about his past and what made him who he was today. The woods brought out a new side of him, a calmer disposition and a more open, accessible manner. "I'm glad you took me here."

"I'm glad you came." His face brightened and he held up a finger. "Do you hear that?"

"Hear what?"

When he didn't answer, she listened to the rustle of leaves, the call of a bird, and…was that wind? No, it was too constant it had to be "Water. Falling water."

Giddiness filled his eyes. "We're close."

The further she pushed on, the louder the rushing of water became until it roared like a rainstorm. Had they hiked all the way to Niagara Falls? They broke through the tree line together, standing upon a cliff overlooking a massive waterfall. Water cascaded down a long drop into a pool before flowing in white sheets over layers of rounded rocks. It was gorgeous.

Cool mist sprayed Alaina's hot face, and the air smelled fresh with a hint of moss and pine. Lance hugged her close as they took in the sight together.

She was hot and sweaty, and her legs burned, but endorphins flowed through her. A sense of accomplishment, much different than what she got from singing, triumphed inside her. She felt more alive and at peace at the waterfall with Lance then at the end of any concert.

Totally worth the hike.

They found a dry rock and set up their picnic lunch. The hotel had provided small ham sandwiches, juice and brownies for dessert. With the waterfall at her back and Lance beside her, it was the best lunch she'd ever had.

The hike had given her quite an appetite, and she downed two sandwiches before lying back against the rocks to watch the waterfall. Lance packed up the remnants of their lunch and sat beside her, spreading out his legs against hers.

"You said you'd make it worthwhile." She teased him by poking him in the stomach.

He spread his arm out over the waterfall. "This isn't enough?"

She shrugged. "I was hoping for-"

"I know what you're hoping for." He brought his face down to hers and kissed her.

She kissed him back voraciously, grabbing the back of his head with both hands.

He deepened the kiss as his fingers trailed blazing heart down her arms.

Every part of her body ached for his touch. How a man could have such a grasp over her, she had no idea.

"Woohoo!" A shout interrupted the perfect moment.

Alaina jerked up and slid back to her spot on the rock. Somehow she'd managed to lay right on top of Lance in the process of kissing him.

Oops. Like she'd take it back.

Two hikers stood on a cliff across the waterfall peeling off their clothes. A third one splashed into the pool below.

Annoyance spread through her. She looked away in disgust as one of the guys flashed his bare behind. Why couldn't they have arrived ten minutes later? "Are they crazy? That must be freezing."

Lance smiled as if amused. "You've never seen a naked man before?"

"I have." She gave him a knowing look. She wasn't a naïve virgin who blushed when someone said the word *penis*. "I just don't want to see *them* naked."

"Well, neither do I." He jumped to his feet and offered his hand. "Come on. We've got two and a half more miles to hike back to the hotel. We should get a move on if we want to get back before dark."

She narrowed her eyes. "Are you saying I'm slow?"

"No." His smile held a hint of guilt as if she'd aught him in a lie. "I'm saying we'll take our time. You know, enjoy the scenery."

The other two guys jumped in after their friend. Alaina turned around as the first one started to climb the rocks below. "Anything's better than this."

As they hiked back, suspicion clouded Alaina's perfect day. She went over their kiss at the waterfall. Lance's passion for her was clear. But, he almost seemed relieved when the hikers had showed up. Was he one of those wait until your married type of guys?

Surely he would have told her that by now. He didn't strike her as that type.

So why was he holding back; sleeping on the loveseat and breaking off their kisses?

A sliver of doubt cut her heart. Was it her? The dream came back to her, when Mrs. DeBarr told her she didn't know what true love was. And she didn't. All her life she'd put her career ahead of her personal life, and every guy she'd met picked up on that pretty quickly. Sure, they were attracted to her, and they'd have fun together for a while. But, no one wanted a diva for a wife.

Lance must be too noble to go all in for a woman he had doubts about. But, Alaina was willing to take the risk. One way or another, she'd get to the bottom of it. She wasn't going to waste another night.

***

Brett secured his bowtie in the mirror. Behind him, Alaina emerged from the bathroom in a silky red dress clinging to all the right places- places he ached to touch. Her red hair had been curled and teased around her face, bringing out her high cheekbones and sharp, green eyes.

How he was going to restrain himself, he had no idea. It was hard enough at the waterfall. Visions of them lying naked, their clothes strewn over the rocks flashed in his mind. If those hikers hadn't showed up, who knows how far they would have gone? In any other situation he wouldn't mind. But, posing as someone else, he couldn't bring himself to go further.

She'd be sleeping with Lance, not with him.

"Ready for dinner?" She smiled, meeting his gaze in the mirror.

He turned to face her. "If it's anything like last night, I wouldn't miss it."

Her eyes grazed over him from head to feet. "You look so hot in that tux."

Damn. Her boldness turned him on. He offered her his arm. Best they leave the room before they miss dinner altogether. "Come on, we don't want to be late for our reservation."

She took his arm. Did a hint of disappointment cross her face?

"You're looking stunning tonight as well."

"Thank you."

Her smile touched him deep down, caressing his soul. How could he deny her his affections? How could he deny himself?

The hostess showed them to a table overlooking the back deck. Golden lights tapered off into darkness as the hill dropped away to the valley down below. Large windows always gave Brett a sense of peace, like a lifeline to a place where he could feel whole.

131

This hotel reminded him so much of what he'd left behind. Sure, the scenery drudged up painful memories, but at the same time, they reaffirmed who he was and what he wanted out of life; walks in the woods, a simple home in seclusion, and the woman sitting across from him.

"What are you thinking about?" Alaina sipped wine from a rounded glass.

He sipped his own wine, tasting the pungent, sweetness of ripe apples. Very different than his corner store beer. "The outdoors. How I've missed it." At least it was the partial truth.

He had to remind himself she came from the city, and that was a big part of who *she* was. But, he'd grown to like New York as well; his construction job, Phil's friendship, the majesty of the opera house.

Alaina put her glass down. "I can see why you enjoy the outdoors. Hiking cleared my mind and gave me a sense of physical accomplishment. I'd never walked so far in my life!"

"Geez. I hope you're not sore." The last thing he wanted to do was turn her off to his favorite pastime.

She gave him a challenging glance. "Not at all. I'm stronger than I look."

Her inner strength always shone through, but today it radiated like sunlight all around her. "That's what I love about you."

She glanced down and put her hair behind her ear. He'd never seen her so shy.

"Thanks. Not everyone sees it that way. To some people it comes across as arrogance."

He reached across the table and touched the back of her hand. Her skin felt smooth and cool. "Not to me."

She placed her hand on the table carefully as if playing a key card in a game. "I wouldn't mind coming back here, even having a summer cabin of my own someday."

Glasses and spoons clinked around them as light-hearted conversation filled the room, but for him the background noise dimmed. He froze, grasping the whole meaning of what she was implying. Alaina was not subtle. This wasn't casual dating. She was the real deal. She meant to try for a life with him. But, would she still have him if she knew who he really was?

The waiter showed up, giving Brett a reprieve.

"Are either of you interested in dessert?" The young man reminded Brett of Phil at an earlier age. He had the same round nose and kind brown eyes.

Alaina looked at him with a questioning gaze.

Brett didn't want to prolong this conversation. It was getting too serious too soon. "I'm stuffed. Unless you'd like something?"

"I'm eager to get back to our room." Mischief crossed her eyes and Brett swallowed hard. How was he going to resist her?

She wiped the smirk off her face and turned to the waiter. "Long day of hiking."

As if that's what she meant.

"Of course. I'll get your check." The waiter hurried off.

Alaina paid the check with her gift card from the raffle. He didn't like having her pay for everything from her own winnings, but he couldn't afford any of it on his construction worker's pay. At least not until he became a supervisor.

A supervisor.

Brett blinked in surprise. That was the first time he'd thought ahead and included New York in his future. It was the first time he'd wanted more- not for himself, but so he could take care of Alaina, so he would be worthy of someone like her. Like it or not, she was slowly working her way into his heart.

They made their way upstairs. Alaina took out her key and opened the door.

Brett stopped at the threshold. Could he go in there and trust himself?

"Well?" Alaina smiled curiously. "Are you going to stand there all night or are you coming in?"

Brett ran a hand through his hair. "It's just that-"

She stepped toward him and placed a finger on his lips. "I don't bite. Well, maybe a little."

He bet she did. Desire rose inside him and he pushed it down. He took her finger from his mouth and held her hand in his. "I'll sleep on the couch."

Confusion and disappointment crossed Alaina's face. She pulled away from him. "Why? Is it me?"

Her reaction crushed him. Rejection was the last thing such a beautiful and talented woman deserved. "No, of course not."

She shook her head. "What is it?"

He shook his head as shame and guilt overwhelmed him. What could he tell her?

"Fine." She walked past him, unable to conceal the hurt in her face. "I'll get you your own room so you don't feel uncomfortable."

Uncomfortable? The last thing he felt with her was uncomfortable. "Alaina." He grabbed her hand. "That's not necessary."

Tears welled in her eyes. "What is necessary? What do you want?"

Her vulnerability cut straight to his soul. An overwhelming urge to make her happy came over him. He wanted to comfort and protect her, to make her feel complete. He wanted her.

Brett leaned down and kissed her tenderly. The kiss didn't come from passion, it came from a deeper, more profound place- the beginnings of love.

She kissed him back, running her hands across his back and up his neck, lighting him on fire. They stepped away from the door, and he closed it with one arm never breaking their embrace.

She pulled him toward the bed and they fell backward, rolling in the soft furs. She pressed against him, awakening a deep primal urge he couldn't ignore. Soon, he'd lose himself in the moment, and he wanted to so badly.

Brett pulled back, gasping for air. "There are things you don't know about me."

She pulled his head down toward her and started unbuttoning his shirt. "I know you're a good man, and that you care about me.

That's enough."

CHAPTER SIXTEEN

Return to Reality

Alaina woke up to bright sunlight and bliss. She nuzzled closer to Lance, feeling his warmth against her bare skin and taking in his manly scent. She wanted to stay here forever, lying in his embrace while he slept.

Her fingers trailed along his strong jaw, feeling the rough stubble. She'd never seen him so peaceful before. Something dark lurked beneath his stoic composure, and she'd taken the darkness away, if only momentarily. Someday she'd ask him more about that cabin in the woods and why it was so dear to him, but for now, she was content with what he could tell her.

She could be patient.

Lance was not an open book, but that's what drew her in; his mystery. She enjoyed the challenge. She knew exactly how her fellow musicians ticked, but this guy was a puzzle aching to be solved. If only she had all the pieces.

He opened his eyes and took in the sight of her beside him. A smile spread across his lips. "Good morning. How do you feel?"

Such a gentleman to think of her needs first. "Perfect. Content. And you?"

He smiled, but that same darkness she'd seen in him all along surfaced for a second. "I feel like I don't deserve this."

"You do." She laid kisses along his arm.

"You don't regret anything?" He sat up, leaning against the wooden headboard.

"You should know me well enough by now." She teased him, running a finger along his bare chest. "I know what I want and I go after it with no regrets."

"That you do." A cloud passed his face. The mood had changed from sexy to somber.

Alaina sat up beside him. "What's wrong? Are you hungry?"

He shook his head. "Come here. I just want to hold you for a little longer."

Alaina's heart melted. *So sweet.* She laid back down beside him and he wrapped his arms around her like it was the end of the world and he didn't want to let go.

***

On the ride back, Alaina stared out the window, watching the falls colors pass in a blur of red, orange and yellow. Wistful melancholy spread through her. Would they come back there someday and talk about the first time they'd been together? Or was it the last time she'd see the place again?

"I think my favorite part was the hayride." She glanced across the limo seat.

Lance smiled, but he'd lost his earlier confidence. He turned back to his window without another word.

Alaina sighed as emptiness hollowed her stomach. Every subject she broached dropped dead in the air. Was he anxious about his job the next day? Tired from the weekend? Or worse- did he regret the time they'd shared?

She couldn't believe that last thought. *No.* He'd held her in that bed like he was afraid someone would come in and take her away. He'd been so passionate, so loving the night before. She'd seen him open up more in a few hours than in all the time they'd shared so far.

It was something else; that darker side she couldn't explain. Could it have to do with Mrs. DeBarr? Or maybe with the cabin he'd lost in the woods?

She bit her tongue, suppressing all the questions she wanted to ask. *Give him time.* If she came out in full force, she might scare him away. She'd come on too strongly before. That's one of the reasons why she lost that Italian tour guide. She couldn't control men; she could only control her own actions.

Slowly the trees gave way to more urban areas with shopping centers and restaurants on the side of the highway. Traffic picked up around them, and before she knew it, they were entering New York. The White Mountain Lodge seemed like a world away, a hazy dream.

If only they'd had one more day.

As the skyscrapers surrounded them, uneasiness spread through her like a fever but she wasn't sure why. Lance still sat next to her. He hadn't said anything to make her think he didn't enjoy their time. So why did she sense something slipping through her fingers?

The limo driver dropped her off first, pulling up to her apartment building. Even though the sun had set behind them, it seemed too soon to say goodbye. Too much lay unresolved between them. She'd gone into the weekend wanting to solidify their relationship, but it felt even more slippery than before.

Lance walked her to the door as the driver unloaded her luggage. "Thank you for a wonderful weekend." Wistfulness accompanied the sincerity in his voice as if the weekend was their first and only one.

"You're welcome. I'm looking forward to the next one." She raised both eyebrows in expectation.

"Of course." He placed a light kiss on her cheek. "Until then."

Alaina stared as he walked away. When was *then*? Was she going to let him get away with such a lame goodbye?

"Lance?"

He turned around.

She dug her fingernails in the strap of her purse. What could she say? The ticket! Of course. "The performance is Friday night. I'll leave the ticket at the box office in my name."

He put his hand over his heart. "Thank you. I wouldn't miss it for the world." He turned back toward the limo and opened his door.

She cupped her mouth with her hand to project over the din of traffic. "So, I'll see you then?"

He nodded. "I'll be there."

He stepped into the limo and drove away.

Alaina's shoulders sagged as disappointment punched her in the stomach. Her performance was whole week away. How could he wait so long to see her after the special night they'd shared?

Was he married to his job?

If so, what had she gotten into?

***

Brett's chest ached as the limo drove away. Why the hell hadn't he restrain himself? Their night together had been perfect- everything he'd ever dreamed a night like that should be. She was 'the one.' That part was clear. But, an average Joe like him didn't deserve a goddess like her. Especially after lying about who he was.

Had he ruined his chances because he couldn't stop loving her?

All he'd wanted to do was reciprocate her affections. But how could he tell her his true identity after pretending to be someone else for so long? She would have never picked a construction worker for a boyfriend. He'd just weaseled his way into her bed.

She'd never forgive him.

Every minute they spent together only delayed the inevitable. Why the hell should be draw it out any further?

Damn Mrs. DeBarr and her cancer research. He would have been much happier had he never met that old woman. That way, he'd never have to break Alaina's heart.

Brett dug his fingernails into his fisted hand. Even if he wished he could take it back, he knew he wouldn't do it. Meeting Alaina was the best thing that had happened to him since the fire. She reawakened him to the living world. She showed him there was life after so much tragedy and loss.

He walked down the moldy carpet of the hallway in his apartment building. Coming back to his crummy apartment after such luxury reminded him of who he really was. Who was he kidding? Could he really live that life of caviar, expensive wine and opera fundraisers?

Only one more time. For Alaina.

Brett opened the door and collapsed on his old couch. He'd promised her he'd come to her performance, and he would. Only after he saw her sing would he tell her the truth.

CHAPTER SEVENTEEN

Prize Students

"Okay, let me have it; your heroes and villains along with their themes and your story lines." Alaina stood by her desk, curling her index finger toward herself. "Pass them in."

As each student walked by her desk and stacked their tattered notebook papers, Alaina smiled, proud. These kids had come so far; from never watching an opera to writing one themselves, and so had she. Never in a million years would she have thought she'd enjoy teaching. Coming back to work gave her the distraction she needed from thinking of a certain backwoods loving guy.

She'd made a pact with herself not to check her phone and not to say his name. Even in her mind. If he wanted to wait all the way until Friday to see her, then she shouldn't make him such a priority.

Jackie walked by and handed in a stack of papers.

Alaina ruffled through them. "What's all this?"

She'd dyed her hair purple and red over the weekend, and surprisingly, the highlights brought out her dark eyes. "My opera. I got a little ahead of myself this weekend and started tying all the themes together."

Alaina studied the first few pages. "This is excellent."

"Nah. It's stuff I made up."

"But it's really, really good." She checked Jackie's wrists, but the girl wore a long black sweatshirt. Alaina hoped she'd stayed busy enough not to avoid making any new marks. "You're still coming to your lesson after class, right?"

"Yeah." Jackie's voice sounded weak and unsure.

Alaina gave her the death stare reserved for her own opera villains. "You'd better, because I'll be waiting for you."

Jackie nodded and returned to her desk.

John walked by and handed in three sheets of paper.

Alaina glanced down at the scrawled notes and names of the rap stars who populated his inner city setting. Although not as brilliant as Jackie's, his ideas showed creativity and a great deal of effort. Seeing him reminded her of something she'd purchased over the weekend.

"John, I'll need to see you after class."

He glanced up in indifference. Today he had three earrings in one ear. Was one new? "What, am I in trouble?"

"No. I have something for you."

His eyebrows rose in surprise. He still wore the same sweatshirt she'd seen him wear all last week. Did he ever wash it?

Alaina played her gift down, trying not to raise his expectations too high. "Nothing big, just something I found."

He nodded and walked back to his seat.

He'd probably never wear the black sweatshirt she'd bought in the gift shop at the White Mountain Lodge, but it didn't hurt to give it to him anyway. Just in case.

After class, Alaina read through the homework assignments as the clock ticked closer and closer to her rehearsal time.

Jackie was ten minutes late. Alaina would have to leave in the next fifteen if she was to reach the Met in time.

As she stuffed the assignments in a manila folder, Jackie knocked on the door.

"Come in." Alaina couldn't hide her anger from her voice.

"You're late."

"I know." Jackie didn't take her backpack off. "I don't want the lessons."

Her words slapped Alaina in the face. Why would someone so talented refuse excellent training? "Why not?"

Jackie bit her fingernail. "Because you're wasting your time."

"I am most definitely not." Alaina stood eagerly. "Even if you haven't been practicing, we can still go over the warm ups."

Jackie shook her head and continued to chew on her nail. "What good is it going to do?"

"It's going to make you better. Teach you how to sing correctly."

"For what? So I can sing at someone's birthday party?"

Alaina put both hands on her hips. "For college."

Jackie rolled her eyes. "Pft. I'm not going to college. I'm going straight to work at my Uncle Dinny's gas station."

"Is that what you want?"

Jackie flinched before she could hide it. "It doesn't matter what I want, it's what I have to do."

Anger and frustration rose inside Alaina. This girl had talent, she had a chance in a lifetime and she was going to throw it all away.

Before Alaina could stop herself, she reached out and grabbed Jackie's arm and turned over her wrist. New marks cut into her skin. "Is this what you have to do, too?"

Jackie yanked her arm back and cradled her hand against her chest. "You have no right."

"You're right. I don't. I'm just the substitute teacher. But, it looks like your parents and your school nurse aren't doing their jobs, so I'm stepping in."

Jackie backed toward the door. "You're just the substitute teacher. You can't tell me what I should and shouldn't do."

Alaina crossed her arms over her chest, trying to peel away the hurt to get to the heart of the matter. "No, but I can give you a chance at something better. It's up to you to take it."

"I can't." Jackie left and slammed the door behind her.

Fury broiled inside Alaina along with a sense of helplessness. If she couldn't get through to this girl, then she'd failed. Rubbing her temples, she checked the clock.

Holy Batshit.

Rehearsal started in ten minutes.

***

Tamino ran across the stage from the serpent as Alaina stumbled into the theater. She took a seat in the back, hoping no one noticed her late arrival.

"Looks like you lucked out. Altez decided to start from the beginning again." Bianca spoke from behind Alaina, leaning on the back row of seats.

Lance's advice came back to her. If she was going to confront this diva, then now was the perfect time. Alaina turned toward her and waved her over. "Hi, Bianca. If you're right, you have some time before you're on. Why don't you have a seat?"

Bianca stared as if she'd just offered her poison. Then, she waltzed over and sat two chairs away. "If you're trying to invite yourself to my early rehearsals with the others, forget about it."

"I'm not at all." Alaina turned so she faced her nemesis head on. "I'm busy at that time anyway."

"Good." Bianca readjusted the straps on her pink sequined shirt. "Because there isn't any more room."

Alaina took a deep breath. *Here goes nothing.* "What do you have against me? What did I ever do to you?" It felt oddly therapeutic to question her out loud, as though she'd kept their mutual animosity private for so long that it had begun to fester.

Bianca straightened in surprise. "You don't remember?"

Alaina shook her head. "Remember what?"

Bianca smiled, but there was no joy in it, only bitterness and irony. "Of course you don't remember. I was just a freshman, and you were the hot singer on the block."

Alaina tried to remember back, but nothing of consequence came to mind. Her ignorance made her the butt of a cruel joke she didn't understand. "What?"

Bianca tapped her pink fingernails on the seat as if remembering something Alaina had apparently said five years ago back brought the annoyance back in full force. "They'd just announced the results of the soloist competition. You'd won, of course, beating me by a tenth of a point. I came to congratulate you."

She swallowed hard. "You were wearing a teal prom-gown type of dress, and I'd worn something my mom had made from some cheap fabric we'd found at a craft shop. She'd passed away that year, and that was one of the last things I had that reminded me of her. I'm sure you never thought to ask, but I was a student at Heart House my senior year because, as a single dad, my dad couldn't afford the tuition for my performing arts school. Anyway, you turned to me and you said, 'you'll have better luck next time if you dress for the part.'"

Bianca shook her head. "After that day, I knew we'd never be friends."

Horror stung Alaina in the gut as shame burned her cheeks. Bianca, a student at Heart House? She would have never guessed. "Bianca, I'm sorry. I honestly don't remember saying that."

Bianca shrugged. "Of course you don't. I'm sure you don't remember calling Isabel Grant a 'vibrato crazed shrieker' or Terence Smith 'math-challenged.'"

Alaina covered her mouth with her hand. The vibrato comment she did remember, but she hadn't thought of it until now. As for Terence, he never made his entrances because he never counted his measures, which had annoyed her. But, she should have been better about keeping her opinions to herself. She didn't know so many people had heard her say that. "I'm a different person now. I'd never think or say those things today."

"Unfortunately, calling people names is like singing a bad note. You can't take it back." Bianca stood and walked toward the stage,

145

leaving Alaina to gawk in in thick, sticky guilt.

Alaina deserved everything that had come to her. She had been a shallow, cold-hearted diva in her early career. She'd been spoiled with her wealth always thinking about her own career and not those around her. She'd never thought to volunteer her time until Altez had practically shoved it down her throat.

Remorse came crashing through her. She felt like Bianca had held up a mirror and Alaina didn't like what she saw.

She'd missed so much - friends she could have had- people's lives she could have touched. How many girls like Jackie passed through Heart House only to end up in dead end jobs- or worse- in the emergency room at some hospital because of a suicide attempt or drug overdose?

Karma had a way of coming back to everyone. It was about time she did something to turn it around.

After rehearsal, Alaina walked up to the podium. "Mr. Vior."

The old man glanced down through his spectacles. His wild, white hair framed his head. "Ah, Alaina. What can I do for you?"

Okay, don't fidget, speak with confidence and professionalism. "I'd like to talk to you about my volunteer job at Heart House."

"Oh yes, I hear it's going spectacularly well. The principal says the students love you."

"Oh, really?" Surprise bowled her over. After rejecting the other teacher's lesson plan and making them all write an opus, she thought she'd been close to getting fired. "I hadn't heard that."

"You've also been seen at every fundraiser and luncheon this opera has sponsored in the past two weeks." He stepped off the podium and placed a hand on her arm. "I know why you've come to me. You've done enough to improve your image. I'll talk to the principal and have him hire another substitute. You can focus on your singing." He started packing up his briefcase.

Alaina shook her head and followed him. "That's not what I want at all."

Altez raised his white eyebrows in confusion.

"I want to keep teaching as long as possible." Certainty hardened her resolve. "In fact, I'd like to stay. Have them put me anywhere they need someone."

He looked at her in confusion, like he wasn't sure who he was talking to. "You're sure about this?"

Alaina nodded. "I've never been more sure."

Altez scratched his head. "It seems Roxanne and I have misjudged you."

Alaina shook her head. She couldn't have him thinking something that wasn't true. "You haven't misjudged me. I was quite a diva. But I've changed."

"Very well. I'll send your request to the principal immediately." He snapped his briefcase and started walking down the aisle.

She chased after him. "There's one more thing."

He stopped and turned around. "Yes?"

"I thought the Met could establish some sort of working relationship with Heart House. You know, provide free tickets to their students, and even have contests that include them in our programming."

Altez pursed his thin lips. "Free tickets? For a whole school? That's a big step."

Alaina stood her ground. "You told me yourself no one is going to come and watch me sing if I'm such a diva. Well, no one is going to support this opera house if we don't do something to inspire today's youth. Kids are growing up listening to rock and rap, and Justin Bieber. If we don't keep classical music alive and accessible, there'll be no opera at all."

Altez chewed his bottom lip as if considering her words.

Alaina straightened. She was a community leader now. Her opinions had as much weight as any, and she believed in this cause. "I'll do whatever it takes. Even if it means donating my own money to buy their tickets and sponsoring the competition."

Altez regarded her with newfound interest and something more, something she'd hadn't seen him have for her as of yet; respect.

"What are you thinking we should do?"

CHAPTER EIGHTEEN

Deal Breaker

Brett checked his watch as he sat in the coffee shop near his construction site. He'd ordered a small coffee for the use of their table, but his stomach was too acidic to drink it.

One more clandestine meeting and I'll end this whole fiasco once and for all.

The door jingled as it opened, and Mrs. DeBarr came in wearing her signature long black leather coat. She ordered a latte and a Danish, and joined him at his table.

"Brisk autumn day, isn't it?" She took the cover off her latte and blew across the foamy milk.

Brett didn't have time for small talk as his shift started in less than fifteen minutes. "How is Mr. DeBarr?"

She glanced down into her latte. "Unchanged."

Even though he knew her answer, it still hurt knowing that poor old man lay in the hospital waiting to die. Brett ran his fingers over the rim of his cup. "I'm sorry."

"It's not your fault. You've helped me tremendously." She smiled and broke off a piece of her Danish to share.

Guilt came over him as he refused the piece of Danish. He'd

grown fond of this old woman, and he didn't want to hurt her, but now his relationship with Alaina came first. "I'm sorry. I can't attend the luncheon this weekend. I can't pose as your son any longer."

She nodded, chewing her Danish. "I thought you might change your mind after this weekend. To tell you the truth, I'm surprised you kept your word this long."

"I wanted to tell you first so you'd be able to defend your actions if word spread."

She waved her hand. "I'll be fine. It's not the first time someone put a misidentified item on the auction block." She winked at him.

Brett smiled. Misidentified was right. "But what about the money for research?"

Her face sobered and she shook her head. "Even though I won't stop fundraising, I know I'm too late. I'm not stupid, just stubborn. All I can do is keep pushing forward. It gives me a purpose."

He reached across the table and squeezed her hand. She felt so brittle, so small, like her husband in the hospital. If he could find a wife that loved him that much, he'd be happy. "I'm sorry I can't help you any longer."

She tapped his hand. "You've done enough. It's wrong for me to get in the way of your relationship."

Relief trickled through him. He didn't think this conversation would go so smoothly. "After the performance on Friday, I'm going to tell her the truth."

Mrs. DeBarr nodded and studied his face. "How do you think she'll take it?"

"I don't think she'll tell on you." He ran his fingers up and down his cup, feeling the warmth of the liquid inside.

"That's not what I'm afraid of. How will she feel about you?"

Brett shrugged. "I don't know. But I have to do the right thing."

Mrs. DeBarr wrapped the other half of the Danish in a napkin and pushed it across the table toward him. "If it's true love, she'll forgive you."

Brett pushed his chair back and stood. There was nothing else to say. All he could do was wait until Friday and see. "I have to go to work."

Mrs. DeBarr stood and gave him a hug. "Take care of yourself, son."

Son.

After tossing his coffee, Brett took the half of Danish and left Mrs. DeBarr in the coffee shop. He knew he wouldn't eat it, but he couldn't bring himself to throw it out. Mrs. DeBarr had given him a taste of what it was like to have a mother again, and he wanted to hold onto that as long as he could.

Phil sat on the curb with a middle aged woman with brown hair tied back in a bun. She wore a cute plaid peacoat and black knee high boots. They laughed together, eating sugar doughnuts. He spotted Brett and raised his hand. "Hey, there's the man."

"What?" Brett wasn't in the mood for conversation.

"Brett, my man. Meet Sarah."

Sarah? As in *The Sarah*? Brett shook his head in surprise and offered his hand, feeling honored.

Sarah wiped her doughnut fingers on her coat and shook his hand. "Don't mind the powdered sugar."

"I won't." Brett marveled in awe of his friend. Sarah was prettier than he'd thought, with delicate features and cute dimples in her cheeks. She matched Phil well. And she loved his favorite doughnuts. How much better could you get?

"So, you're the one responsible for getting this stubborn mule to give me a call?" She laughed and poked Phil in the belly.

"I can't take all the credit." Brett smiled at Phil. "My friend here wouldn't stop talking about you, so I figured it was the only way to get him to shut up."

Phil punched him in the arm. "Don't you have to be getting back to work?"

"I do." Brett rolled up his sleeves. Even though the autumn air was brisk, the sun had come out, and the day warmed up pretty quickly. "I'll leave you two lovebirds alone."

"Just a sec." Phil gestured for Sarah to wait for him as he followed Brett to the construction site.

"She looks really happy. Good job, man." Brett gave his friend a sincere smile. "I'm happy for you."

"Thanks, but that's not why I'm here." Phil looked around uneasily. "Some pretty blonde came by the site this morning right before you got here. Said she was looking for someone named Lance DeBarr. I thought you might know who that was."

"Shit." Bianca was onto him. Brett shoved his hard hat down over his eyes and glanced around from under the plastic ridge. "Thanks for letting me know."

"You betcha." Phil whispered under his breath. "If there's anything I can do to help-"

"There's nothing you can do, thanks. I'm going to resolve all this on Friday at Alaina's concert. All I can do is lay low until then."

"Okay, good luck, man." Phil clapped him on the shoulder.

"Thanks." Brett sighed as he walked to the back of the site. Hopefully he'd find something to do away from the street where anyone could see him. As much as he dreaded Alaina's reaction, Friday couldn't come soon enough.

***

Alaina stood in front of her class and used her knuckles as a drum roll on her desk. "I've talked to the conductor of the opera along with the president of the board, and I'm able to offer everyone in the school free tickets to my opera performance this Friday."

Everyone applauded, and she held up a finger, waiting for silence. "That's not all. I've submitted all of your opera ideas to the conductor, Altez Vior. He's going to choose the one with the most promise and you'll start working with the composition teachers at Julliard to perfect it. Because…" she did another drum roll. "The Metropolitan opera, along with the orchestra will perform somebody's opera next season. He'll announce the winner before Friday's concert."

Gasps filled the classroom. Some of their mouths dropped open.

"No way." John shook his head. Alaina was proud to see him wearing his new sweatshirt.

"You've got to be kidding me." Another girl shouted from the back.

Jackie hid her face. She hadn't made eye contact with Alaina since their argument yesterday. Alaina watched her with concern. She thought the good news would cheer her up.

But, she couldn't bring it up in front of class. Sighing, Alaina turned to the chalkboard. "Onto today's lesson. Harmonic progressions that mirror the plot. When you should use a major chord versus a diminished seventh."

After class, as she packed up her purse, the classroom door opened and Jackie came in.

"Jackie. I didn't expect to see you after school today."

"I know we don't have a lesson planned." She picked at a string hanging from her sweatshirt. "I wanted to apologize about yesterday."

Alaina wanted to throw her arms around the girl, but she restrained herself, holding her hands at her sides. She'd already scared her away once. "Apology accepted."

Jackie kicked her boot against the floor. "I guess what I want to say is, I thought about what you said. Whenever I'm focused on my music, I don't feel like I have to..."

She glanced down at her arms.

"Cut yourself?" Alaina gave her a hard look.

Jackie nodded. "I want to try."

Hope rose inside Alaina. She hadn't failed. "You mean you want to continue lessons?"

"If you think it really will help me get into college."

Alaina gave her a warning stare. "That means leaving Dinny's gas station behind."

Jackie laughed. "He'll get over it."

"Good." Alaina pulled out one of her books. "Today we're doing an exercise my teacher taught me when I was about your age."

Jackie raised both eyebrows, her backpack still on her back. "You mean, right now?"

Alaina winked. "I've got fifteen minutes, and we have a lot of work to do."

CHAPTER NINETEEN

Bianca's Revenge

Alaina adjusted her costume in the mirror as nerves ran up and down her spine. She'd prepared for this day all her life with hours of practicing, singing lessons, competitions, and rigorous studies. So many things hinged on this night and it all started in five minutes.

Was she ready?

Alaina touched up her makeup- this time using a newly bought lipstick that Bianca couldn't have gotten her hands on. After checking her dress was properly fitted for the zillionth time, she tiptoed backstage and stood with the other members of the cast.

The audience chatted beyond the curtains in a din of subdued conversations. Alaina pulled an inch of the fabric back and scanned the crowd. All the seats were full. In the second balcony she could make out the students in her class along with others from Heart House. Pride surged inside her, calming her anxious nerves. They'd come to support her.

It should have been enough, but she searched the audience for one more familiar face.

Lance.

As much as she'd coached herself not to let him matter so

much, she still hoped beyond words he'd come.

Altez took the stage, and the audience quietened as he began his speech. He thanked all of the major donors and the president of the board.

Alaina's thoughts drifted back to Lance. He hadn't called her all week, but she couldn't say she was surprised. He'd been running hot and cold this whole time, and his unpredictability had become the only predictable thing about him. If only she had more of the pieces to the puzzle.

Altez's voice pulled her back to reality. "I'd also like to thank Alaina Amaldi for organizing a new competition for the students at Heart House."

Alaina snapped up. This was it. He was going to announce the winner.

Altez turned to the cast backstage. "Alaina, can you join me?"
What?

All of the cast members around her perked up and smiled. Tamino, along with a few of the flamingos pushed her forward. "He's asking for you."

Alaina walked on stage, and the audience applauded as if she'd already sung her part in the opera. But, they weren't clapping for how well she could sing, they were clapping for the work she'd done. Altez greeted her with a peck on the cheek. He whispered in her ear. "I wanted to make sure you were a part of this."

Shock ran through her, along with gratitude and a warming sense of pride. She'd done this for the students, and it gave her immense joy, beyond anything she could have won for herself. "Thank you."

The conductor pulled an envelope from his pocket as he explained all the details of the competition. "And the winning opera is... *Lady of Venice* by Jackie Anderson. Jackie, if you're out there, will you please stand up?"

Alaina searched the balcony, fear and hope rising inside her. Had she come? Would she accept the prize?

Way up in the second balcony, the students of Heart House shouted Jackie's name. In the back row, Jackie stood, cringing in embarrassment and hiding her face with her hands. When she pulled them off and looked at the crowd, she beamed with happiness. She spotted Alaina on stage and waved. Alaina waved back thinking of the first time she'd seen her in class and how far she'd come, how far they'd all come; even herself.

Elation coursing through her, Alaina followed Altez off stage and to her dressing room as the orchestra tuned. Jackie's piece would be performed at the Met next season. The opportunities to meet influential people and develop relationships with the composition staff at Julliard were numerous, not to mention how great the accolade would look on her college application.

Alaina had made it happen. She'd never felt so good about herself, and that pride gave her the confidence she needed to perform at her best. So far, the evening was going spectacularly well.

A knock sounded at her door.

Oh no. Was it Bianca coming to throw her off kilter?

Nothing Bianca could say would ruin this night. Alaina pulled her hair back behind her shoulders. "Come in."

Lance walked in with a bouquet of roses, and her heart somersaulted. The entire night stopped, suspended in time, and the world blurred around her. Nothing else mattered. He'd come.

"I hope I'm not intruding. I wanted to wish you good luck before your performance." Lance stood at the door like a shy delivery boy, waiting to be invited in.

"My gosh! Come in, come in!" Alaina took the roses and threw them aside, wrapping her arms around him. She nuzzled her face into his chest, smelling his familiar pine scent. "I'm so glad you came."

Blissful peace came over her as he held her in his arms. All the time they'd been apart melted away.

Lance pulled back to meet her gaze. "You look gorgeous. This must be Pamina's dress."

"In all its glory." She pulled away and twirled so the chemise skirt fanned out around her legs.

Lance smiled. "Gorgeous."

She stepped back toward him and touched his suit with both hands. Clean and crisp. She wanted to take it right off. "You don't look bad, yourself."

His face sobered and he took a deep breath. "There's something important I have to tell you after the performance."

Alaina's heart skittered. "Why can't you tell me now?"

He kissed her forehead tenderly. "I don't want to distract you before your big night."

"You're already guilty of that." Alaina laughed, but when she saw he wouldn't budge, she nodded, trusting him completely. It had to be good news. He wouldn't have come otherwise. "All right."

"There you are!" Bianca butted in, pushing by them in the doorway. At first Alaina thought Bianca was coming for her, but she pointed a finger at Lance. "You little liar."

Fury boiled within Alaina. How dare she ruin this perfect moment? She moved between them and turned to Bianca. "Get the hell out of here."

A smug grin plastered on Bianca's face. She looked over Alaina to Lance. "I visited your office yesterday, trying to book an appointment for a consultation. Turns out, you weren't there. Someone else was sitting at your desk. Why don't you tell her your real name?"

His real name? What? Bianca must be smoking crack. Alaina turned around, facing Lance. "What's she talking about? Why do you have another guy doing your job?"

Lance's face slackened. He dropped his arms to his sides. "Alaina, I'm sorry. I was going to tell you after the performance."

Her stomach dropped to the floor. "Tell me what?"

"That he's about as close to Lance DeBarr as a rat in the sewer." Bianca strutted between them. "The real Lance DeBarr never attended the auction. *His* name is Brett Robinson, and he's a construction worker- a lowly grunt who's never worked a day on Wall Street in his life."

Alaina shook her head, denial building a wall inside her. "No. I've met his mother…"

Lance/Brett stepped forward. "It's true."

All the clues came rushing back to her- his wallet, his reluctance to talk about work, the strange way he consulted with Mrs. DeBarr, his mysteriously private life during the week. Hurt crashed through her. She should have known he was too perfect to be true. Her lower lip quivered. "Why?"

"Mrs. DeBarr's son couldn't attend the auction, and she asked me to stand in his place. I know it was wrong, but I wanted to help her because" He winced like he couldn't come clean and say the truth. "…it was for a good cause"

"A good cause?" Was he trying to make it seem right? He'd lied to her the whole time they were dating. "Was sleeping with me for a good cause as well?"

Bianca slipped out the door. "I'll leave you two alone. Alaina, you're on in twenty minutes."

Alaina let her leave. Her anger with Lance/Brett eclipsed her anger with Bianca.

He took her hand. "I wanted to tell you the truth so many times, but Mrs. DeBarr made me promise."

"Maybe on our first date, I would have understood, but after everything we've done together…" Her thoughts trailed off. How could she ever trust him again? She couldn't.

Alaina hardened her resolve. "Get out."

"Alaina, please, let me explain."

She handed him the roses and pushed him out the door. "You already have."

Alaina slammed the door behind him and collapsed to the floor, clutching her stomach. Her insides retched and her chest ached. She'd just lost the love of her life. But she'd never had him in the first place, because that Lance didn't exist. Emptiness overwhelmed her, threatening to swallow her whole.

On in twenty minutes? She could hardly stand, never mind sing in German. This time Bianca had found the ultimate sabotage; driving a knife right into her heart.

I will not let her win.

Alaina may not have love, but she had her singing, she had her pride. All of her students were sitting out there waiting to see her, and she couldn't let them down. Pulling herself up, she wiped the tears from her face.

***

Earth shattering pain wracked Brett as he left Alaina's dressing room. She'd been so happen to see him, and now she never wanted to see him again. He'd lost the one person who brought him joy in his life, the only one he'd let in since the fire.

He'd never let anyone in again.

The hurt was unbearable, shuddering through his chest until he couldn't breathe. He braced himself against the wall several times on his way to the lobby, fighting against the crowd going in. He reached the door, and his knees weakened.

How could he leave her?

Responsible for her anguish, he'd be a coward to leave her on her performance night. He'd promised her he'd be there to hear her sing whether she wanted him there or not.

Brett walked back inside the theater and took his seat holding his flowers to his chest. Alaina had chosen the best seat in the house; the first balcony overlooking the stage. But he deserved anything less than the best. If he'd ruined her debut performance, he'd never forgive himself.

The curtains opened, and a man ran across the stage, fleeing a serpent. Even though he spoke German, the translation appeared on a screen on the back of the chair in front of him.

"Help me, or I am lost!"

The audience laughed around Brett as a tear rolled down his

cheek. Opera wasn't anything like Vikings shouting at the top of their lungs. The music transcended language, speaking directly to his soul. He was lost as well, but his serpent was remorse and it would take more than three women in giant headdresses to vanquish the vile beast.

Brett waited on the edge of his seat for Alaina to enter as Pamina. Instead, one of the servants of the Queen of the Night showed the picture of Pamina to Tamino.

Tamino held the frame in his hand. "The beauty of this woman has captured my soul."

The melody soared in a giant leap, then ended with a soft turn of phrase. So gorgeous. Brett remembered the first time he'd seen Alaina across the street. Words could not express what he'd felt, but Mozart captured the emotion perfectly in the music. Love at first sight. It existed back then in seventeen hundred and ninety one, and it existed today in the modern world.

Tamino held the picture up. "Something stirs in my heart when I gaze upon this heavenly face. I can't say what it is but it burns me like a flame. Is this love?"

Had it been love with Alaina? Brett was begging to think it was. He'd never cared so much about a woman. Mrs. DeBarr had told him if it was love, Alaina would forgive him. But he could hardly see her talking to him again.

Brett shifted in his seat, anxious. It had been twenty minutes and Alaina still hadn't entered. The scene ended, and with a stir-ring of violins. Brett shifted in his seat. How long were these operas anyway?

Alaina took the stage, looking more beautiful than the first day he saw her. She sang, and her voice soared, pure and resonant. He couldn't believe someone so talented had given him a second's thought.

Because she thought you were someone else, you idiot.

Surely, she would have passed him by on the street had she seen him in his construction gear. And she had, that fateful day before

Mrs. DeBarr pulled up in her limo. Alaina had looked directly at him, then got into her cab without another thought.

That's the way it should have been.

The longer the opera went on, the harder it was for Brett to watch. But, he couldn't tear his eyes away. So much of the storyline reminded him of his own situation.

On stage, a temple priest instructed Tamino to remain silent to prove his love for Pamina. The scene reminded Brett so much of Mrs. DeBarr asking him to remain silent about his true identity. Sure, it was different circumstances, but Brett related to Tamino's inner turmoil as Pamina approached him and he could not speak.

So many times he'd wanted to tell Alaina the truth. If only he'd had the courage to do so earlier. But it would have meant him breaking his promise to Mrs. DeBarr. Would Tamino break his vow?

Brett sat on the edge of his chair, beads of sweat forming on his forehead as Tamino turned his back on Pamina. Suddenly everyone on stage faded into shadow, and Alaina took the center, bright light streaming down on her hair, lighting it on fire.

"Ah, I feel love has left me, forever gone." The achingly beautiful tone of her voice reached Brett's ears, and it was like she sang to him alone, calling him out on everything he'd done.

"Nevermore will I feel bliss." She reached towards the highest balcony. The sorrow welling up from within her was too poignant to be fabricated. It sung to his soul, pulling tears from his eyes. She was Pamina singing about Tamino, but she was also Alaina singing about him. Alaina had turned her emotions for him into a stunning performance. Maybe the performance of her career.

She ended the aria with a gorgeous cadence, and the spotlight darkened. The audience cheered, standing on their feet. The orchestra had to stop and wait for the applause to die down before resuming the performance.

Brett sat back in his seat, speechless at the enormity of what he'd just lost. If that wasn't true love soaring from her heart on stage, than what was?

CHAPTER TWENTY

Parting Gift

Alaina lost her balance as she walked off stage and fell onto a flamingo.

"Whoa, are you okay?" The flamingo girl helped her stand.

"I'm not sure." The enormity of the emotions coursing through her mind threatened to knock her unconscious. Had she sung all the words, all the pitches? She couldn't remember. All she could feel was the power of her sorrow overcoming her. She'd embodied the role so completely; she'd become Pamina.

The girl tilted her head, her flamingo beak pointing to the side. "Do you hear that?"

"Hear what?"

"They love you." She brought her to the edge of the stage and pulled back the curtain. Most of the audience had stood from their seats- which was unheard of in the middle of a production.

Alaina stared in bafflement. "That's for me?"

"Yup. Soak it in."

Alaina couldn't believe it. Had she sung that well?

"Come on, let's get you to a chair. You look like you're going to pass out." The girl led her backstage. "Do you need anything before you go back on?"

"No. Thank you." Alaina collapsed in a folding chair as the girl left to prepare for her scene. Shock and disbelief rattled her senses. All of those people clapped for her. She'd gotten a standing ovation during her debut performance at the Met.

If she hadn't still been entrenched in the aria's emotions, she would have been on cloud nine.

A few feet away, Bianca fastened her black headdress beside a mirror with a miserable frown on her face. "Congrats. They love you."

"Thanks." Pity softened Alaina's heart. She actually felt sorry for her. By exposing Lance, or should she say Brett, Bianca had meant to ruin Alaina's performance. But the betrayal had given Alaina the substance she'd needed all along, taking her performance to the next level.

Must suck to have your plan explode in your face.

Alaina chugged some water from her water bottle and her dizziness cleared. "By the way, I owe you one."

Bianca glanced at her with distrust. Black lipstick suited her so well. "For what?"

"For telling me the truth." Alaina stood and held out her hand. This had gone on too long. "Truce?"

Bianca stared at the hand as if it were diseased.

"Listen, I'm sorry about what happened between us, and I'd like to start from scratch."

"Pft." Bianca smoothed over her dress. "As if. I don't have time for this. I'm going on in five minutes."

Alaina quelled her rising frustration, breathing deeply. This would be harder than she thought, especially since her performance had drawn the first standing ovation. The old Alaina would have thought Bianca wasn't worth her breath, but after hearing about her past and her time at Heart House, Alaina couldn't give up on her. "We both know you and I aren't going anywhere, so we might as well work together. I'd like to have a fellow colleague come with

164

me to my scholarship meeting with Altez next Monday. I'm sure you'd have some good ideas."

Bianca glanced at her with suspicion. "You don't mean that."

Alaina nodded, still holding out her hand firmly. "I do."

She'd gained favor with the conductor, and the smartest move would be to befriend her rival. Bianca may not like her, but she wouldn't jeopardize her career for personal feelings. At least, that's what Alaina bet on.

Bianca pursed her lips. She reached out and shook Alaina's hand. "Very well. Truce."

Behind them the stage director called for the Queen of the Night.

"Good luck out there." Alaina smiled.

"After what you just did, I'm going to need it." Bianca gave her a half smile and took her position back stage. It was the first compliment Bianca had ever given her.

An uneasy peace had settled between them, but it might be the start of a working relationship. Alaina sipped her water, preparing for her next scene.

She'd still watch her back. Just in case.

***

After the performance and two encores, Alaina walked back to her dressing room with three bouquets of flowers in her arms. She'd sung better and better with each entrance, and Altez had come up to her at the end and kissed her hand. For a moment, she'd forgotten all about the fake Lance.

Until she saw his roses lying outside her dressing room door with a note.

Really?

He couldn't just deliver them again and hope everything would be all right.

She picked up the roses and moved to throw them away when the note caught her eye.

Dear Alaina,

You were marvelous. I enjoyed every minute we spent together.

From a sewer rat to a superstar,

Brett.

She'd told him to take a hike. So why had he stayed for her performance? Did he think he could still have a chance with her after lying the whole time?

Alaina paused over the trashcan. He had told her he'd wanted to tell her something after the performance. Was he going to tell her the truth?

She'd never know. Should she care?

She shouldn't, but the wounded part of her soul that already missed him did. Hardening her nerves, she threw the roses away and took the other three bouquets home with her. She didn't need anything reminding her of Brett.

CHAPTER TWENTY ONE

Truth

The next morning, Alaina opened her apartment door and stared at the newspaper at her feet. This was it; the make it or break it moment that would define the rest of her career at the Met.

She opened the New York Times and flipped right to the Arts and Entertainment section. The top headline was a review of the opera by Ernest Theodore the second, the leading music critic in the world.

Hands shaking, she braced herself and read.

"The Metropolitan's interpretation of the wonderfully popular *The Magic Flute* comic opera by Wolfgang Amadeus Mozart is a must see. Altez Vior lights the orchestra on fire as the maestro, and the stage sets are beyond the best I've seen. But…"

Alaina's spotted her name coming up and her heart dropped to the floor.

"…the most outstanding element of this magical performance is Alaina Amaldi's performance of Pamina in a stunning, daringly sorrowful rendition which came straight from her soul with such unusual intimacy."

Alaina grasped the paper to her chest. Ernest Theodore called her 'stunning.' He thought she was daring? He'd realized she was singing straight from her soul?

She should have jumped for joy, called everyone she knew, and hosted a giant bash at the richest club in town. Instead, Alaina quietly closed the door to her apartment and placed the paper on her kitchen table.

The victory was empty. She had no one special to share it with.

If only Lance had been real.

But he wasn't. He was Brett...what had Bianca said his name was? Brett Robinson, some kid of construction guy.

Wait a second.

Alaina remembered back to the day she'd had her audition. Hadn't she seen a wide shouldered construction hunk with shoulder length chestnut hair staring at her from across the street? Had it been him?

She turned on her laptop and carried it to the couch.

Who was this Brett Robinson anyway?

Despite her logical reasoning to let the matter drop and be done with it, she typed in his name and almost dropped her computer on the floor.

Local Logger Loses Both Parents in Forest Fire. The headline was from the Daily Tribune in northern Maine. Alaina read the article, learning of his family's logging business, the cabin he'd built with his father, and the tragic fire that had swept the northern forests in Maine last year, obliterating everything meaningful to Brett.

Alaina rushed to her kitchen drawers and riffled through old receipts, napkins, and melon scooping spoons. She found the Project Wish pamphlet they'd given her at that first auction to show where her money would go. *Thank you so much for choosing to donate to Project Wish. Your money will benefit the victims of tragic events such as hurricanes, floods, fires...*

Fires.

Was that the 'good cause' he'd referred to?

Guilt swept over her. He'd helped Mrs. DeBarr because it

benefitted the charity he believed in from his own experience. To refuse to help her would have been against everything that had happened to him. He probably thought he'd go out with the buyer of the date once and never see her or him again.

Then, Alaina had bought the date and turned his plan upside down. He hadn't expected to want to see her again, or for them to fall for each other. But they had. At least she had.

A knock sounded at her door, and Alaina whirled around. Who would visit this early on a Saturday morning?

Brett? Even though she understood him better, she wasn't ready to see him yet. She didn't know if she wanted to see him again at all. She'd been so certain last night, but after reading the article and putting all of the pieces of the puzzle together, she still hadn't made up her mind.

Alaina tied her bathrobe around her waist and peered out the peephole in her door.

Mrs. DeBarr stood in the hallway wearing her long leather coat and pearls, her hair curled and her makeup done as though she'd been up for hours.

What the heck was she doing at her door?

Alaina undid the lock. "Mrs. DeBarr? What brings you here?"

The old woman folded her hands in front of her. "I've come to formally apologize."

"Apologize?"

"For leading you to believe Brett Robinson was my son. Now are you going to let me in, or do I have to get down on my knees and beg?"

The last thing Alaina wanted was for one of the Met's greatest sponsors, and a frail lady in her seventies to feel unwelcome. "Of course, come in, come in. You'll have to excuse my apparel." She showed Mrs. DeBarr to her living room. It was too bad she'd let her place to go hell over the past few weeks. Worn clothes hung on the backs of chairs, and dirty dishes had piled up in the sink.

"Dear, after how you sang last night, you deserve to walk around

169

in your pajamas all weekend." Mrs. DeBarr took a seat in the armchair by her sofa.

Alaina sat across from her. "You were there?"

"Of course I was. You were marvelous. In fact, a little *too* marvelous. I can't help but think some of that sentiment was a product of the situation I put you two in."

Alaina glanced down, unable to accept Mrs. DeBarr's apology on Brett's behalf. "I certainly understand you trying to find a stand in for your son for the auction. But Brett is a grown man. He could have told me the truth at any time on any of our dates. It was his decision to lie." And to sleep with her under the guise of another man- but she thought she'd leave that part out. Mrs. DeBarr didn't need the X-rated version.

The old woman held her gaze with a drop-dead stare. "He had no choice."

Alaina shook her head, not wanting to accept another story. All it did was create more confusion in her heart. "What do you mean? You didn't hold a gun to his head...did you?"

Mrs. DeBarr laughed, fingering her pearls. "No gun involved. I assure you." Her eyes grew sad, and she frowned, looking ten years older than her age. "I was greedy and lonely, and I wanted a son who had the time for me, a son who could help me fundraise. So, I took him to meet my husband at the hospital. I told Brett every minute he stayed my son bought more research for my husband's cancer. How could he have said no?"

Alaina's heart broke all over again. If what Mrs. DeBarr said was true, Brett had lied to her for all the right reasons. She'd punished him for acts of charity, and for falling for her in the process, when it would have been much easier to brush her off. "Why are you telling me this?"

Mrs. DeBarr reached across the space between them and took her hands. Even though her fingers were small and frail, she had a hearty, determined grasp. "Because he cares about you more than you know. He'd wanted to tell you the truth all along. I got in the way."

All of the walls Alaina had built broke down inside her, and tears welled in her eyes. "I was so mean to him. When I learned the truth, I kicked him out."

Mrs. DeBarr nodded. "It was a normal response. I'm sure he still wants see you, that's if you're still willing to have him. He is a construction worker, as you know."

"What someone does has never made a difference to me." Alaina chewed on her lower lip.

"Then, what really matters, my dear?" Mrs. DeBarr searched her eyes.

Anger rose inside her, still fresh from last night's embarrassing display in front of Bianca. "Honesty's a big one."

Mrs. DeBarr wiggled her pointer finger. "He'd planned to tell you the truth all along."

Alaina played with the tie of her bathrobe, wrapping it around her finger. "I also want someone I can have fun with. Someone who accepts me for who I am."

The old woman spread her hands. "I don't usually share my opinion on such matters, but in this case, I have to say he's the one."

The one.

Her stomach hollowed out. "That's what the psychic said at the White Mountain Lodge." Alaina ran her hands through her hair as realization hit. "Brett couldn't acknowledge it because she'd said his parents had died too soon- of smoke inhalation and he was still pretending you were his mother. But, the psychic was right. And she had a message from them from beyond the grave."

Mrs. DeBarr's eyes widened. "What was the message?"

Alaina's skin prickled with goose bumps. "'She's the one.'"

Mrs. DeBarr pursed her lips. "Was she, by any chance, talking about you?"

Alaina covered her mouth with her hands. "I think she was."

Acceptance, guilt, and hope stormed through her. "I have to find him. I don't even have his number or know where he lives."

Mrs. DeBarr sat back in the chair and threaded her fingers together on her lap. "Now that, I can help you with."

CHAPTER TWENTY TWO

Offer

Monday mornings always hit Brett with a cold dose of reality, but today ranked as the number one worst. The cloudy sky rained icy drizzle, he didn't have anything in his apartment to eat for breakfast, and he'd lost the love of his life. Staring at the Met all day was the last thing he wanted to do.

"I take it that telling her the truth didn't go so well?" Phil opened his package of powder doughnuts and stuffed two in his mouth.

"Nope." Brett checked the truck. A whole new shipment of planks to unload. Today was his lucky day.

"So what happened?" Phil offered him a doughnut, like that was going to fix everything.

Brett took it anyway. "Before I could tell her, that blonde woman who'd visited the site the other day came over and spilled the beans."

"You mean the one asking for the guy named Lance?"

"Yeah."

"Shit." Phil shook his head. "Tough luck, huh?"

"Like she would have liked me any better if I'd told her the truth?" Brett shook his head. "I'm a construction worker, and she's an opera star. She wouldn't have given me the time of day if she'd met me for real."

Phil glanced at the sky and furrowed his brow, looking like a Greek philosopher who liked doughnuts. "You can't know that. From what you've told me, she sounds like she'd looking for Mr. Right not Mr. Rich."

Brett shrugged, knowing his friend was right, which made the wound in his soul ache so much more. Alaina had been everything he'd hoped for. She wasn't a snobby diva, but a kind-hearted person who didn't mind hiking in the mud, teaching kids music, or throwing rocks in a stream.

A black limo pulled up to the curb with the license plate DeBarr. Brett's chest tightened. "Oh no, not Mrs. DeBarr again."

"Maybe this time she'll ask you to impersonate some senator to get some kind of cancer research legislation passed."

He raised an eyebrow at Phil. "What have you been watching on TV?"

"Nothing. With the stories you tell, I don't need it." Phil winked and stepped aside. "I've got to finish my doughnuts. Good luck, man."

The limo door opened, and a glorious head of red hair came out. She wore the same red blazer she'd worn on their date, along with super sexy skinny jeans, revealing her long legs, and of course her new hiking boots.

Brett's hopes soared at the same time as the pain of rejection came back in full force.

Alaina turned and caught his gaze as the other construction workers around him whistled and hollered.

Brett turned around and gave them all death stares. He felt oddly out of place in his old jeans, orange vest and construction boots. But, he was done with putting on a show. This was the real him, and she'd have to accept it whether she liked it or not.

He hoped she liked it. Otherwise, why would she be here?

"Alaina?"

She crossed her arms. "I have a proposition to offer you. I was supposed to go to a luncheon with this guy named Lance DeBarr. Well, it turns out he has no idea I exist, so I was hoping you'd stand in his place."

Brett smiled; she always managed to cheer him up, even on a gloomy day. "Does this mean I have to auction myself off again on another date?"

Alaina pursed her lips as if considering it. "Not if you agree to go on one with me."

Brett couldn't take it anymore. He had to drop this little game. "You mean you forgive me?"

"You know what they say about second chances." Alaina reached in her pocket, took out a rock and handed it to him. "Just don't throw it at the cars."

Brett held the rock like it was a diamond of hope. "What made you come back?"

"Oh, you know, your typical visit from a fairy godmother." She jabbed her thumb at the limo."

Brett laughed. "She can be very persuasive."

"She can." Alaina's face turned serious. "But even before Mrs. DeBarr visited me, I'd looked you up the morning after my performance. I know about what happened to your cabin in Maine, and I'm sorry about your parents."

Brett glanced away. Could he talk about it? If he wanted to be with Alaina, than he had to try. "I came to New York to get away because I couldn't stand the hurt."

"I know." She took his hand. "I want to build another cabin with you someday, when you feel like you can go back. You make me happy in so many ways. You've shown me there's more to life than opera. When I'm around you, I'm a better, more rounded person. You've taught me how to laugh at myself when I fall over a rock or get scared by a bug. You've given me advice on how to talk to the people who have always despised me and make them respect me. You're the dose of modesty I needed all along. I'm sorry I ever doubted you."

Humbled by her admission, Brett shook his head, speechless. "I'm just a construction worker, Alaina. I don't work on Wall Street. I have no money for fancy weekend getaways or caviar."

"I don't want all that, Brett." She cupped his chin with both her hands.

Hearing her say his real name sent shudders of bliss through his body.

Alaina pulled his head down to hers. "All I want is you."

"I want you, too." Brett stared straight into her eyes. "You challenge me in ways I should have challenged myself. You've shown me I can have a life after tragedy. That I have a place in this big city- and it's by your side."

They kissed, and the construction workers hooted behind them. Brett picked Alaina up and twirled her around. All around them, the presence of his parents surrounded them with love.

He'd build that cabin with her, and they'd live there in the summers when the opera was taking a break. Maybe someday, he'd start another logging company when the forest on his family's lands grew back. The future shone brighter than it had since the fire. Finally, with Alaina's help, he could move on with his life.